Praise for Humanity's Grace

"In this mysterious and moving novel in stories, infused with pitch-perfect details of everyday life, ordinary people absorbed in their personal worlds of pain and loneliness seek connections with those around them, often strangers, in a web of relationships that becomes something extraordinary. Characters move in and out of each other's lives, thoughts, and memories, their stories coalescing into a surprising and satisfying conclusion that ultimately, through various small acts of redemption realized along the way, does define a kind of fragile and yet tenable human grace." — Jeff Fearnside, author of *Making Love While Levitating Three Feet in the Air* and *A Husband and Wife Are One Satan*

"Montgomery writes using the skills of a weaver; presenting rough fibers of life, sadness, and regrets, along with the soft thread of tenderness, love, and human relationships to create these stories; like a loom displays its almost finished right angles of cloth." — Doug Erickson, co-author of *Jefferson's Western Explorations: Discoveries made in exploring the Missouri, Red River and Washita*

"Life's great moments are often quiet. Dede Montgomery has written a book made up of such moments, allowing readers to ponder and reflect on life." — Tom Hallman Jr., a Pulitzer Prize winning journalist and author

Other books by Dede Montgomery

The Music Man
Beyond the Ripples
Then, Now, and In-Between

Humanity's
Grace

Humanity's Grace

Dede Montgomery

Bink Books
Bedazzled Ink Publishing Company • Fairfield, California

paperback 978-1-949290-72-1

Cover Design
by

Bink Books
a division of
Bedazzled Ink Publishing, LLC
Fairfield, California
http://www.bedazzledink.com

"A single act of kindness throws out roots in all directions, and the roots spring up and make new trees."
—Amelia Earhart

Stories

The Moment After

WHAT HAPPENED IN that last moment before the moment after? Paul's hands had shot up to cover his ears, their trembling fingers adorned by nails chewed down to the quick. The blaring sirens had frightened him, blocking out images and memories from only moments before, irretrievable to him now, hours later. Rough knuckles and fingers had grabbed at his wrists, leaving them red and sore.

"Say something!" Garbled verbal commands loudly punctuated the blur of noises, foreign to him in that moment, as if coming from extraterrestrials.

"What did you say? Why are you here?"

These statements were undecipherable to him in those moments, blank dialogue bubbles floating above cartoon characters. *Why are they yelling at me?* Instead, Paul blindly struck out, terrified.

"Put your hands up and move away." A voice penetrated through the cacophony of sirens, traffic, and voices.

Paul shook then, vibrations searching to find a route out of his body. "Please leave me alone," he whispered, as he dropped to the ground, shrugging into a fetal ball. "I was trying. I was trying to help." The cement was cold and the smell of old piss emanated from its cracks. His unconscious mission now was only to take up as little space as possible and pray for a miracle. To disappear like the magician in a trick from his boyhood, the one he had always wanted to see repeated again and again.

"Get up!" echoed around him.

The voices were loud and angry to Paul, as if shot from a firing line. He did nothing wrong, he wanted to yell but fear immobilized him, making him unable to obey commands.

"Please," he whispered again, believing uniformed people would protect him.

His eyes now locked tight: if only he would awaken as if from a nightmare, sweaty and shaking but soon after comforted by his familiar bedroom. A rented room he knew was safe, where he could walk to the grocery store and to his job as an animal tech supervised by a woman who never raised her voice. Oh no, he remembered. The yells, sirens, and blinking lights short-circuited the neurons in his brain. Paul was merely trying to help, and he expected to be comforted, not accused.

"Get up!" he heard again, a foot nudged his hip, his body slumped on the ground as if he were a drunk blocking a store front, he who could count on one hand the number of drinks he'd ever tasted.

"Please. Leave me." He was infantile, without the ability to move body parts—feet, knees, hips. *Why wouldn't they leave him alone and give him quiet?* His spirit had bolted from compassion and sadness to a terror that immobilized him.

"What are you doing here?" a different man in uniform asked in a quieter voice.

"Hurry up!" a voice yelled from beyond.

"Nothing," Paul gasped.

He kept his eyes clenched shut, frightened as he desperately sought his private world. A safer world. Away from these things he did not understand. He was helping the man, the man who was alone and hurt. *Where did the man go?* The noises and lights interrupted his focus.

Paul forced his eyes open to peer toward the flashlight beam: pointed at another crumpled figure on the sidewalk. Paul barely recalled making the 911 call. Or did he? Then rising abruptly, frightened when the flashing lights and sirens disrupted the peace. A peace, only a few minutes before filled with comfort and his own prayers, surrounded by distant sea gull croons and tug boat air horns. The crumpled figure was the man who was hurt: before the sirens, lights, and yelling. *Why was the man in uniform yelling and the sirens screaming while the other man didn't stir?* Paul's eyes wandered to the deep red stains on his shirt sleeves. He rubbed one, then stared at his hand, damp with blood. Paul squeezed his eyes shut again and remained on the ground, incapable of doing anything in such pandemonium. His body ached suddenly, pain tore through his arm and his head throbbed.

"No! No!" he cried, snot dripped from his nose and mixed with the saliva from his mouth, hanging from his face before it dribbled toward the ground. Paul closed his eyes once more as he shivered, withdrawing to the strong arms that grabbed him, walked him toward the patrol car, asking questions Paul could not decipher in his terror-filled state.

THAT WAS THEN. Now, he was not sure if any of the before mattered. Had he been in this spot two hours or two days? He was numbed, unable to tell if he was hungry or needed to pee, he rubbed his fingers along the hem of his softened flannel shirt in a failed attempt to comfort himself. He was in a stupor yet, knocked out by fear and noise and lights, not heroin or crack like others who might be captive nearby. Before, the officers acted as if following a course of action only they were privy to and his brain could not follow their thinking. Now, none of those moments before seemed to matter. Whether it was yesterday or today, was the crumpled man's breath gone forever, heart stopped? Would Paul's own moments enter a void stretching into eternity? Eternity: he remembers when he first tried on that word.

"It can't go on for ever and ever, Mama," he had said to her all those years ago. "Nothing can just keep going."

Now, as a grown man only barely, Paul knew life's moments weren't eternal. His lost moments of before still too foggy to decipher what had happened, silenced by sleep in this dim small room. What had he missed to get landed here? He expected people in uniforms to know things. To protect him. Their questioning of him from before created a seed of odd premonition. Maybe he did know something, but he was too tired to figure it out. He was ordinarily the one who noticed everything and protected others, no matter how small: how could he not know what they believe he did? Neurons in his brain were misfiring, improperly directed and scattered ineffectively as he blindly looked desperately around the darkened room for a savior. Help me, he pled silently. His head throbbed as he accepted something to be terribly wrong.

Voices from elsewhere seeped into the room, and the beeping of radios trickled through the wall. He wished for light, not flashing lights, but soft yellow beams to lift the dimness of this room rather than the stark single bulb overhead. The room's dampness smelled like dirty socks, and the buzzing in his ears from exposure to loud noises competed with muffled voices for attention from his brain. Paul shivered again.

"No. No," he muttered, barely audible, worn out and lacking space to store expanding bundles of fear.

He looked down at the cuffs on his wrists, then closed his eyes as he slouched back against the smooth, cold concrete wall. *Why did they put these on him?* He was not a bad person like the criminals on TV.

Paul's terror was interrupted by the sound of footsteps and clinking keys outside the door. Whoever it was turned a key in the lock and the door opened, creating a triangular path of light into the room. A figure approached him, and Paul could tell it was a man wearing a uniform. He was now afraid of uniforms. The man walked toward him, reached out and lightly tapped his shoulder.

"Get up," he said calmly.

As Paul rose, pain flooded his thighs and back, even though his wrists and feet felt numb. *Has he been transformed into somebody else?* He squinted at the man who shepherded him toward the door but Paul was distracted as he tried to open his sticky eyelids. He drew his eyebrows up in an effort to open his eyes wide, trying to clear his vision.

At first, all he could see was the dappled triangular pattern of light on the tiled floor. He couldn't take his eyes off its perfect symmetry filled with angles and holes. But a firm push directed him, moving him away from the pattern of light, even though he wished to stay in its safety. Yet, Paul was a man to follow rules, and now he moved his feet on his own to where he is directed, first right foot, followed by left. *Where is he?* He was less frightened but still confused. Once he left the room and entered a brightly lit hallway, he identified a different stench of despair, tinged with Lysol. Now he was moving easily, no push needed to prod him further. He shuffled along the corridor, stiff from sitting, as daylight streamed in through windows on one side. He looked outside and spied stunted pine trees before mimicking the movement of the man ahead of him. The man stopped at a door. Paul was jolted by the sound of a buzzer and the clank made by the door as it was unlocked and then opened. He wanted to tell them to make the noises stop, but he couldn't get words out. He wondered if the loud noises and flashing lights swallowed his ability to speak.

"Go ahead," the man said. Quietly. Almost friendly. *Did he imagine all the mean voices from before?* Paul glanced at him, questioning, before turning to the figure the man nodded at.

Paul wanted to rub his eyes. She was there. He closed his eyes tightly before opening them again to create tears to see more clearly. Was she real? All of his tears had been used up. She rose from a plastic bench. He recognized her, though her eyes looked different: tired and ringed with red. She was the only one to understand him: he knew this now as if for the first time. He knew she was disappointed in him. He wondered if she had given up on him, her only son. He searched her face quickly for the answer before looking down at the floor, unable to handle the intensity of her expression. He was certain she was ashamed, believing he did something wrong. The men in uniform knew. They were supposed to help him, she had always promised. He couldn't remember his mother ever looking at him this way before. Before, she would have made certain to never let him be here. He looked up nervously at her, and her eyes replied: *How could you?* How could he after everything she had done for him. He wanted to plead to her to believe him, she that knew him better than anyone else must believe him.

Now he doubted himself. He wanted to scream: *Help me! Please take me home. Where it is quiet and I can think. Please, Mama. Believe me, trust me. I was only trying to help.* Her tired eyes told him, leftover tear tracks as if permanent scars even though her eyes were dry. "No." He knew her, this mama of his. "That's all. That's it. I can't," her eyes said to him. *Please, Mama,* he wanted to cry out. *Please, Mama. One hug. And then, I will let you be.* He silently prayed, knowing only then he had never prayed before.

As if he had spoken aloud, the uniformed man turned away. Paul's mother looked at the man and her expression changed from sadness and disappointment to curiosity. Had she shrunk since the last time he had seen her, not so long ago? The man in the uniform looked distracted and stepped away from them as if to feign looking out the window. To look out to a cement parking lot and cloudy mist. His mother spoke but her voice was muffled, and Paul couldn't make out the words. Still the uniformed man continued to look out the window. Paul looked down at his hands, pieces of skin red and raw from fidgeting with the cuffs. He forced his fingers together in a memory from the past. Here was the church. Steeple. See all the people.

"No, no, I can't," he muttered as he slowly moved his head side to side. Yet, still the man looked outside.

His mother stepped toward Paul, glancing at the uniformed man who continued to stare outside. His mother turned back to Paul and stood in front of him, staring into his eyes. Was this the end, Paul wondered? The only thing left was this moment. He tried to move his arms but they stayed lifeless in front of him, raw, stiff. She moved closer and he got a whiff of lavender, the laundry detergent he remembered her using. Still, she looked in his eyes. Her expression now told him everything. *If this is the end, I will still love you forever. And hate whatever it was you may have done. To yourself. To me. To us. But in this moment, I forgive you, her eyes said.* She lifted her bare pale arms with their drooping flabby skin, and raised her wrists as she tried to encircle him. This stooped woman was too short and couldn't clasp her hands behind his neck, so instead rested her body against his chest. Paul felt comforted in this moment. Now he smelled cinnamon and remembered rolling out cookies at a wooden kitchen table long ago, using special cookie cutters she let him select.

Paul closed his eyes. No more yelling. No more loud noises circling deep within him. He breathed in, and relaxed into her tiny body, being careful not to knock her over with his bulk. In this moment. Other moments would come, but not in this moment. In this moment, he felt relief tinged with joy. This was their moment.

The Remembrance

THERE WAS NO casket, yet its absence would have surprised no one. If they'd been asked, those who knew Frank would have been amazed to learn a service was to be held at all. If anything, a two-lined obituary in tiny hard to read print, buried in the small-town newspaper. On second thought, probably not even noteworthy enough for the *Astorian*. If it were a bigger city, it'd be ignored entirely.

It wasn't that Frank was an unkind man. He had simply been forgotten. A one-time self-taught auto mechanic who only began working in a warehouse to address mounting bills during a tight economy. And yet people came. A dozen and a half, and at least one who was only curious. Clustered together in a no-nonsense cheaply paneled room funded for public gatherings by the city, or by tax payers, some might argue: the few who knew him, some who heard about it, and the rest who wanted free snacks and wondered. Curiosity, it attracts people in good and bad times.

Nobody in the crowd was visibly grieving, except for Anne. Frank's daughter Anne grieved, even if her mother didn't. A stranger may have wondered if Anne and Monica were kin, sitting next to each other, a bit of resemblance, dark hair and eyes, small wrists, serious expressions. A dedicated detective, though, would wonder: Are they estranged? Few words were shared between the two, and they sat in metal folding chairs far enough apart to create inches of cool void between shoulders and thighs.

Anne would say if someone had the nerve to ask her mother, maybe after first imbibing in a "stronger than lemonade" drink to loosen up, Frank deserved it, Monica would snap how she wasn't surprised after all. Most people, at a farewell occasion like this memorial, would have the good sense to nod, look down at the ground, and move away, unwilling to encourage spite after the abrupt ending of a man's life. Yet, a few were driven by a reckless nosiness, hanging around for more, even when they know they shouldn't. Then, with an audience and after sipping more wine, Monica might continue, "People who spend their lives selling false bills of sale, deserve what they get." Anne could imagine her mom then looking off into the distance at a storm of images reflecting their past. Time-marked snapshots hovering from so many years ago. Only later might she feel bad for what she said.

Anne squirmed in her chair to relieve the cramp in her back from too much sitting, and she shook her head as if to erase this Etch a Sketch of her imagined conversation. The grayness captured by coastal skies infiltrated her mood and enhanced the room's starkness, making a joke of the euphemism "celebration of life." She stared across the room at a vintage porthole clock, a nautical detail not bold enough to add vitality to the event.

Anne couldn't envision articulating a single sentence coherently. Not now. Instead she sniffed back her tears and wiped at the snot before it dripped from her nose, using the paper towel she'd grabbed before locking her car. Memories and thoughts rattled inside her, ravaging her initially calm brain. No matter what memories she unearthed, they dropped her back at the same conclusion she started with. *No man deserved to be killed by someone else. No matter what.* Definitely not Frank. Obsessed with fantasies about his future? No doubt, but this daughter knew him to be kind, albeit frustrated. Misunderstood? Almost always. She set her feet firmly on the floor as if to offset the ever so slight downward slide of her legs on the slippery chair as she stared ahead, barely listening.

Anne wondered if her dad knew his end was happening. Did he have a few moments to come to peace with it or acknowledge its finale? Might he have appreciated living more years than some may have predicted? Those were questions to which she sought answers.

It wasn't only the barebones service and flowers, Anne contemplated, knowing she was unappreciative, but an expectation to eat together and socialize with people unknown to her. A few people had laughed or chuckled upon entering the room: Why should there be laughter, her twenty-four-year-old brain asked? And, who would care enough to spend money to plan this event if not her, his daughter? Anne knew enough about event planning to recognize it took more than a single phone call: tracking people from the past, finding even a no-cost venue, ordering flowers and food, even if it all came from Costco.

As plain as the room was, did that person know to select one with a smidgen of a view because they knew how Frank liked to look out into the mouth of the Columbia River? Anne remembered those few good days as a teen, wedged between memories of school and family, when her dad would remind her what he liked most. To sip his favorite beer—Anne knew it to be the cheapest in the 7-11 fridge—and stare out toward the treacherous Columbia Bar. He might peer out to the spot where, on a good day, one might make out the shadow of Cape Disappointment Lighthouse or the rocky jetties disappearing into the ocean. Out into the expanse of the Pacific Ocean, even on those socked-in coastal days when he had to fill in its expanse from memory. When she was younger she heard enough from her mom to know about his dozens of unfulfilled wishes, too often blaming others for their lack of fruition. Frank was bitter toward many, his father and his ex, and others he claimed who had wronged him. He held chronic pain in his body from years of hard work and banked frustration because of the aches he endured at pittance wages from some stiff. But when he looked out to the Pacific, Frank would always smile.

She tried to re-focus on the guy talking, wiping her eyes, this time with her fingers, wondering if people would be mistaken to think his words touched her. Now she was distracted that the guy reminded her of the scarecrow from the *Wizard of Oz*, the way he gazed out at the audience as if soon the Witch of the West might dart down with a flying monkey or two. Anne tried to be kinder, maybe the guy was nervous, or he shared a poorly disguised despondency. She forced herself to blink away the image of a guy stuffed with straw, knowing even with all the disappointments she had with her dad, she could not accept him to be gone.

When Anne first heard about the memorial she didn't think she would attend. She had deliberately moved away from the part of her life she considered Chapter One. Maybe, instead it was the prologue. A prologue, a bit too long so that you skimmed it so you could get to the good stuff in the first chapter. The trivial details maybe you'd like to know later but unimportant in the moment. The strange thing was, if people knew her early life story they might assume she'd think poorly of herself. But she didn't. Some days she had more confidence in herself than most people around her. And because of this they didn't disappoint her much anymore. She had a job she was glad wouldn't last forever, but at least supported her basic needs for the moment. Her supervisor annoyed her and the research didn't address the most compelling questions about humans, but pulling volunteers together to try to figure it out was better than being assaulted by off-gassing paraphernalia as a Walmart checker, or some other minimum wage job. She garnered together her own way to pay for her life, keeping largely to herself. It was in this state she had decided at the last minute to attend the memorial.

It was only now when the finality of his death struck her. Before, without openly acknowledging it, she had assumed the two would have more time together. Someday. Time for Frank to stop dreaming about things that never could come, and her to feel bold enough to tell him about the past. Now, the opportunity would never come. Instead, she sat in this room with coffee-stained carpeting and pictures of old fishing boats on the walls, and tried to focus on a few words shared about her dad by this man she'd never seen before. The way the guy was talking, Anne wondered if he was some do-gooder who felt bad about Frank, maybe he had seen him drinking at the local dives. Maybe the guy felt bad he'd been killed by being at the wrong place at the wrong time— nobody yet seemed to know the details about why it happened. At least the Scarecrow kept it brief: too much glowing detail about a guy who was just a regular guy, moving like others through the streets of Astoria, would have been asinine. Anne didn't tend to be sentimental, even though deep down she knew her dad wasn't simply another guy.

Anne surreptitiously eyed her mom. Monica was staring straight ahead, not at the speaker but at a picture of a lighthouse on the opposite wall, or maybe through it into her thoughts. Her expression was impassive, her lips, as always, bare of shine or color, her trademark necklace dangling its milky opal stone at the base of her throat, matched by simple opal studs in the lobes of her ears. Not even her daughter could pick up any trace of what her mind held, as bland as if she was watching a stupid ad on the TV she had already watched fifty times. Anne figured her mom was trying to figure out how soon she could leave to get back on the road to Portland and return to what she cared about.

As if Anne had read her mind, Monica looked down at her wristwatch. Then, as if nudged by Anne's attention, she gave her a small, albeit fake smile. The smile might have said to stay strong, or just as likely, "Don't worry, it'll be over soon. And we can all get out of here."

There was no body. She had read about wakes with public viewing but expected nothing of the sort for her dad. Anne was troubled not to know what became of it, a pauper cemetery or morgue? If she'd been a better daughter might she have ensured he was cremated, afterward hand delivering the ashes herself to the ocean. Did her mom step up out of some late, deep-found feeling of bounded commitment to make sure his after-death arrangements were somehow better than many they'd shared together? Anne wanted to know: had he ticked off someone after drinking too much or had he finally found the word of God, repented and aggravated someone on a street corner? Or had he only been in the wrong place at the wrong time? Anne had stopped answering his infrequent phone calls earlier in the year, tired of his needing to tell her about this or that dream or promise. She had imagined she could get back to him later, only to now wonder where he was on that last day.

Finally, the guy began to wind down.

"Thanks to all of you for stopping by, I'm sure it would have meant a lot to Frank. And please stick around, enjoy the grub. You know, the food and lemonade."

His words ended abruptly and Anne felt the talk lacked an Amen of a finale. She glanced toward the corner where two oblong wooden tables partially covered by muted flower-patterned plastic tablecloths were set up with food and drink. They probably should have only used one, she thought, its offerings paltry when spread out over both tables. From her chair, she eyed white rolled wraps, probably turkey that had been unrefrigerated for too long. Sparkling water. Shortbread cookies. And a plastic tote of the mentioned lemonade, she imagined. Better would have been to skip the words and the food, go down to the beach or pier, and stare out into the beyond. Anne knew she should be more appreciative of the offerings, but she felt depressed and it all seemed cheap and misunderstood.

Something touched her leg, and she turned away from the table to see her mom stand up and put her arms through the sleeves of her light wool jacket. Monica had given Anne a quick hug when she had come in, a minute late, her lips mouthing a silent, "Thanks," for saving her a seat as asked. Anne had borrowed a friend's car to make the longer than expected trip, forgetting how windy the Columbia River Highway was from Interstate-5 to Astoria, rolling past farm land and wee towns. Her foot instinctively hit the brake as she passed by the town of Westport yet she didn't know why. Now, her mom raised her arms for a hug, but Anne felt numb. She didn't want to share this moment with Monica, believing her to be more relieved than not to have Frank gone. Gone for good.

"Not now, Mom."

"Oh sure," Monica said, her mouth turned down after she spoke. "Well, it was so good to see you, Annie. You look good."

Anne returned the frown, unwilling to remind her again she went by Anne, knowing she didn't look that "good" dressed sloppily in faded jeans and a mostly stretched out sweater she picked up at a thrift store.

"I'm so glad you could take some time and get away. Are you sure you don't want to come stay with me for a few days? Catch up?"

Anne couldn't endure this false cheer. Or worse, if it was real. She loved her mom and mostly got along with her now living two hundred miles apart. But shouldn't her mom be sensitive to how Anne might be feeling, to put all the crap aside and be there for her daughter?

"No, Mom. I've got to get back. I'll call you later this week—sorry but I have to find a bathroom first. Are you going to be here for a bit?"

"Oh, you know, honey. I need to get back. I want to get over the mountains before dark." Monica sighed. She buttoned up her jacket and slung her shiny leather purse over her arm. "It was a lot to get here."

Anne refused to point out the obvious: They both had more than enough time to get home before dark, and Anne's return trip was longer. Monica gave Anne a disappointed look, followed by a perfunctory hug. Anne retreated in the opposite direction toward the marked restroom. She didn't need to pee but craved privacy.

Who were these people? She couldn't figure it out as she believed her dad to have been like a hermit. She was relieved nobody else was in the bathroom. Her reflection stared back at her, and she felt even more the child that her pale, thin face portrayed, no makeup, only single studs in each ear and fully tattoo-less. People she met rarely believed her to be a college grad. She didn't think she cared, telling herself how nobody who cared about her did either. She ran her hands under warm water from the faucet long enough to transform her white skin to pinkish. Unable to pull out paper towels when she jammed her fingers in the dispenser slot, she instead shook her hands and watched the droplets splash the mirror. Anne stared at herself in the mirror again as she wiped excess moisture on her jeans, but knew she needed to get out of the bathroom before someone popped in and flooded the dingy space with small talk.

Anne hungered for the solitude of her car where she could block out her brooding with loud AM radio. But her stomach grumbled and she knew better than to turn down free food. She grabbed a paper plate from the corner of a food table, and scanned the faces of the dozen or so people still gathered, most casually dressed in jeans with rain jackets draped over chairs. Formal dress codes rarely existed in towns like this. How odd to be at a farewell for her father and not recognize a soul! She turned back to the first table and picked up a turkey roll, orange cheese, and wilted lettuce doing little to enhance the flesh covered turkey slices, and wedges of mushy apple and melon before she moved toward a chair across the room. She was curious about the people who turned out, the few who talked quietly now and the remainder who sat alone with faces bent over plates.

As Anne nibbled on her food, she created stories about two of them, the older man in navy corduroy pants and stark white tennis shoes sitting alone with his eyes glued to his plate, and the younger woman across from him who cautiously kept looking from one person to another. *How might they have known Frank?* She bit into the turkey wrap, and her eyes met those of an old woman standing across the room. Anne looked away, not in the mood to be examined by someone else. *Dang. Too late!* The curly gray-haired woman smiled at her and meandered her way across the room until she was standing silently next to Anne. Anne looked down at her plate and heard the woman clear her throat. Anne looked at the woman and smiled politely before she quickly looked away. She began to feel uncomfortable.

"You must be Anne," the woman said at last, quietly.

Anne was startled and looked back at the woman questioningly. She was wearing polyester slacks of a pale blue, probably with an elastic waist like her mom swore she'd never be caught dead in, and a gray cardigan sweater. The woman was short and a little hunched over, Anne didn't have to look very far up into her blue eyes. She looked tired and Anne knew she should give up her chair or get another, but she selfishly wanted to be left to her own thoughts and not engage in superficial chatter.

"I'm so sorry, Anne. I'm sorry." The woman's voice broke.

"What? I mean, how did you know my dad? And me?" Anne said, louder than she meant to, affected by the woman's emotion and startled to hear genuine condolences rather than small talk.

"I didn't. And, I don't, not really," the woman said simply. She smiled, but it was a sad smile. "I wish I had known your dad, Frank. But I didn't." She touched Anne's hand. "I'd love it if you told me about him. My name is Marjorie."

Anne was dazed and couldn't help but to stare at Marjorie dumbly. She had stopped anticipating talking to anyone about her dad, figuring they had heard enough or merely didn't care. She felt disoriented and stared back at the woman, wordless.

"Well, then," Marjorie began, softly, "how about you tell me what you loved most about your dad? You don't have to tell me anything else. Just that. Please? I'd like to know."

The woman's hand was warm on her wrist. Anne hesitated before delivering a hint of a crooked smile. Then she turned and looked out the window. "My dad was a dreamer." Her memories and stories felt private, she worried that if she shared them they would no longer belong only to her. She longed to be alone and able to withdraw deep inside herself. Marjorie pulled her hand back and took two steps backward, and Anne worried she had pushed her away. Now she wasn't sure what she wanted to happen. But instead, Marjorie dragged a chair closer to Anne. As Marjorie carefully sat down, Anne put out her hand to help steady her. Once she was settled, she eyed Anne and nodded. Anne took a breath, then slowly exhaled.

"My dad once told me we would run away together and build our own kingdom, and he would be king and I'd be his only princess. Our first order of business was to plan the menu for the food allowed in the kingdom," Anne snorted a laugh, quickly covering her mouth, embarrassed. This wasn't the right place, she admonished herself silently.

The woman laughed, restraining herself as if not to overpower Anne. "Do tell me. What foods would you allow?" She had a twinkle in her eyes.

"You have to realize I was only eight or nine," Anne said. "But it was apples, chocolate, cheese, bread, and ice cream." The knot in her stomach loosened. "And we decided chocolate sundaes would be required in the morning before school." She giggled.

Her giggles dissolved and they sat quiet for a few moments.

"How did you know about my dad?" Anne asked. *Why would this woman care about these stories?*

"Let's just say I heard about him. And I particularly wanted to meet you," the woman said. She sighed.

Anne looked out the window again and told the woman about her dad's love for the ocean, and why he had moved from Portland to Astoria when she was in high school. It didn't feel right to mention her parent's divorce and his crazy fantasies about finding valuable treasures at the coast someday.

"My son loved the ocean also," Marjorie said. "When he was little I would take him to a beach not far from here in the summer. He would tease the waves. He would run out into them and taunt them as he said, 'I bet you can't catch me!' And then his little legs would run back toward the dunes, and he'd be giggling so hard I was sure they would knock him over!" She laughed. She reached into her purse and turned her head away.

Anne looked down at her feet while Marjorie wiped her eyes with a tissue.

"Do you still see your son?" Anne asked, looking at her again.

The woman turned to her and shook her head. "Not in a little while. I'm sure again. Sometime." She forced a smile, but the twinkle was gone. They sat in silence and Anne picked up a piece of apple and took a bite before returning it to the plate. Mealy. All of the food tasted bland, even if it was free.

"I'm so glad I was able to meet you, Anne," Marjorie said. "I can tell your dad must have been proud of you. Would it be okay to give you a hug?"

Anne nodded. Before she knew it, the slight woman had strong-armed her off her chair and into a hug. Anne's heart beat quickly, and she pushed back at first. Then she relaxed her shoulders into Marjorie's droopy arms. The woman's bony wrists dug into Anne's back, but she gave off a smell of lavender that was strangely comforting. Although unexpected, Anne was reassured to share a moment with someone who seemed to care.

She began to feel uncomfortable in this stranger's arms, thankful her mom wasn't there to tease her later. "Oh, Anne, I see you've started a local chapter of Free Hugs." Anne pulled away and sat on the corner of her chair. "Thank you," Anne said, as she looked back into Marjorie's eyes. She didn't know if she was thanking her for the hug, or something more. "I need to be going. I've got to get back to Seattle." She shrugged. "I work tomorrow."

"Anne." The woman hesitated. "Would it be okay if sometime I contact you? Just to check in?"

Anne was confused, but she liked Marjorie, even if their time together had been surreal. She reached into her bag, took out a pen and old grocery receipt to scratch her phone number on, and gave it to the woman.

"Thank you, Anne."

Anne stood up, pulled her jacket under her arm, and nodded to Marjorie. When she got to the door, she looked back to see Marjorie as she put the paper in her wallet. Her emotions felt mixed up and she wasn't certain she was ready to leave now with this newly acquired unfinished business. As she reached for the door handle, the man who spoke earlier spotted her.

"Anne," he said, walking toward her. "I'm Jim Parker and have known your dad for a few years, but I never got to meet you."

Anne forced herself to ditch the stupid movie persona she had imagined earlier and stared at him. It felt weird not to know her dad had a friend.

"He was proud of you. He'd want you to know that." Jim gave her a nervous look. "I know your dad cared. He did."

"Thanks," Anne mumbled as she pushed open the door.

She wished she could say more, knowing now that Jim knew her dad, but her brain was saturated with more than she could process. The moment she stepped outside and drew salty air into her lungs, she felt something new emanating from muscle memory of bony wrists and soft shoulders. She walked toward her car, and only then understood: It didn't matter that she didn't know why Marjorie cared. Maybe tomorrow she would take that on. But for now, the comfort of shared stories, her hug, and the smell of lavender would get her home.

The Badge

IT HAPPENED LONG ago, before he joined the force. Back then he was certain he would not choose the path others expected of him, ignoring his newly raised doubts questioning the authenticity of youthful memories. As a child and teenager he created the mantra he would be different. He, Calvin, would break the pattern, the mold, this—to him—debilitating inheritance. Today, after evaluating those retrievable moments of the past days, years, and decades, he still believes it was a single event that decided his future. Inconceivably, the action he took to change the outcome he most feared, merely sealed it.

Only now he admits he had been a typical, naïve seventeen-year-old. Two decades later he recognizes the traits and dreads the day his own kids reach adolescence, naivety implanted with pockets of ego, fear, and arrogance. These cocky creatures drift into his life today, thinking he knows nothing. They figure adults around them don't know shit, as he did then. A few with intimate knowledge might assume, like he did, that the assholes around them are the same morons who proclaim in public to uphold what is good and true while in darkly closeted personal lives shove a fist into the ones any compassionate human would expect them to love most: wife and kids. No, he knows now, not all of them. But a conspicuous handful dangerously stereotyping an entire force.

Calvin believes even now his own dad never did understand love. Or compassion. Or any of those traits he would taunt others about back when Cal was small: wimpy, soft, he'd say. He'd get down on the ground and demonstrate ten one-armed pushups and then jump up to caress a rippled hairy bicep as if to illustrate what mattered most in life. He'd use words like fag, poof, and lightweight to describe for Cal the people he despised. And yet, while the biceps rippled to the end, it was his dad's heart that killed him decades before it should have, extra beats and not enough blood flow. This dad of his never made it to retirement when he would have been released from work stressors that continuously spilled into life's non-work hours. His heart burst with dreams of power never attained, and probably—Calvin knows now but didn't then—pain he never shared. Well, before his dad's death, Cal told himself over and over: he would be different.

Yes, he would break the cycle by committing an act considered by his father to be most dishonorable. A deed unimagined to be discharged by an officer's kid, or the two uncles who also carried the badge. Stealing or selling drugs seemed to rank as high as murder in the minds of some of his dad's officer friends. This thing that would have been "the worst thing" might simply be a slight transgression in other families. One of those things some kids try out to test its fit, as if selecting basketball shoes. Yes, odd for him, he now thinks, to have identified this to be the worst when nastier things happened routinely behind the anonymous walls of his own home, not to mention out on any mean streets.

Once, years later after he told a friend about it, his buddy had asked him if he had planned it. Had it been premeditated: a question only a cop would ask. Calvin had immediately responded, no. But later, when he was honest with himself, he knew when it happened he felt as though he had imagined doing it for weeks, maybe years, as if he was following directions and orders precisely written and memorized. It was as if he was fated to do it to prove to himself he would be different. *He was different.* If his dad had ever learned about it he would have near beaten the life out of Cal, making sure he was still conscious enough to hear his angry reprimands. "You idiot! If you're gonna do it, at least be smart enough to get away with it," his sergeant dad would have said. The dad now dead long ago. That dad who never knew about his son's disloyal act.

It had been a Friday afternoon, and although more than twenty years have now passed, Calvin remembers it more clearly than most anything else from that time of his life. It was raining outside, and the sky was darkening so early it had seemed to him, a week before Thanksgiving. The rain came down, heavy clouds leaving salty darkness. Now he gets hung up on a trivial question: why a radio? As if he had any interest in that kind of appliance? Was it the value? More than a pack of gum? The challenge: not quite small enough to fit in a pocket?

Only recently did Calvin understand that he wanted to get caught. The man of today is relieved that he did. He had been wearing 501 Levi's and Keds sneakers, standard fare dressed up by the leather jacket he'd pinched his savings together to buy, getting a good enough deal to also later realize it too had probably once been stolen. Rough, worn brown leather looking more like something you'd find on a gang member coveting *West Side Story* than a kid who bagged groceries at Safeway in a small Oregon town. He was barely shaving back then, looking younger than the girls his age, not yet over-aged from early years shouldering the weight of living with what the neighborhood knew to be a mean cop. A cop who came home to drink and only later yell, tuning out the chatter from his wife and kids.

Yes, Cal knew the time had come to be the one to break the cycle and its unspoken assumption. His dad, his uncle, his brother in training: they assumed he would follow in their steps. But deep down he couldn't believe he was like them. He couldn't do all those things his dad did; exude the macho aura yet hide desperation and despair during dark nights and early mornings. He felt trapped by expectation, yet terrified to share the fears with anyone, all of it sweeping him up on that afternoon, that single rainy Friday afternoon.

He was seventeen and had no business walking into Radio Shack, not a kid to have spending money to do much of anything with in those days, or interest in what lay on the store's shelves. Teens who saved for things like stereos and cars, he knew that to be something pretended only on movies and stupid television shows. That wasn't to say he even wanted any of it—not then. He had stayed late at school that day, a straight kid catching up on schoolwork. Embarrassed to admit to his few friends at that time he didn't mind it much, school. School felt fair. He knew what to expect—a routine and system different than what it might be later that evening at home.

He was the last to leave the school library, the librarian had cleared her throat as she pulled her things together for the evening, first inching from shelf to shelf as she pushed her hand along the book covers, straightening the shelved volumes as if packaging the library for evening silence. Then she hovered near the light switch by the door and looked toward Cal. He quietly thanked her, and after walking down the hallway, slipped out the back door of the school, hoping it wouldn't set off some alarm he didn't know about. He stepped into the late fall air, and walked on to what was referred to as downtown, even if it wasn't much. He doesn't remember now if he was so late to leave school because he was procrastinating what he planned to do next, or if he had lost track of time.

Before he entered the shop, he searched for a cop car on the street, knowing its presence would stop him from entering. Seeing none, he pushed through the door. His arms jerked in surprise at the sound of the chime marking his entrance, and he took a deep breath to calm himself. It was otherwise quiet in the shop, those days of the recession when stores would close earlier than today, but before Amazon ruined profit-making for small local retailers. The guy at the counter looked up and nodded expectantly, his expression changing to bland disinterest as he took in Cal. Probably ignoring him because he was young, clean-cut, and white. Would have been different, he knew, if he looked different.

Cal's sneakers squeaked on the floor as he turned to walk down a far aisle, almost as if he knew exactly what he was looking for and where it was located, rather than deliberately moving out of view of the clerk. He had only been in the shop once or twice before with his grandfather when he was younger. He walked the aisle to the back of the store, his pounding heart interrupting his ability to focus on the wares lining the shelves: batteries and car speakers and devices he couldn't identify. Cal had never been one of those guys to talk incessantly about music or cars. When he reached the end of the store he proceeded back up the middle aisle, only then spotting the item he knew he was meant to find. His purposeful hesitation caused his feet to be rooted on the shiny linoleum tile, and he reached out to grab a black Sony radio and jammed it into his side jacket pocket. When it didn't fit he pulled it out, glancing up toward the clerk even though he knew it made him look guilty, and pushed the radio under his jacket mimicking a lumpy potbelly.

He was terrified to have been so stupid not to have thought it out more carefully. Frozen for a moment, he knew the tentative kid he had always been would pull the radio out and return it to the shelf with the cheap devices of that time. It was easy to steal back in those days, Calvin sometimes reminisces, so much trust leaving gadgets for the handling and taking unlike today with miniscule devices locked behind cabinets adorned with alarms ready to beep and stores under the watchful eye of hired security guards.

Yet, after those few seconds elapsed, it was as if a gate slammed down: eliminating his opportunity for redemption. He hesitated too long, and the moment was gone, securing his choice. As if in a trance, he did the only thing he could envision, pretend. Cal ignored the fear accumulating inside him, producing sweaty beads on his forehead and at his crotch. Instead he willed his actions to imitate one who didn't give a shit, as he slowly sauntered toward the front door, blissfully unaware of the scanners and alarms prevalent now. Cal lifted his sneakers carefully off the floor as he walked, trying to reduce their squeaks. He wondered if he should buy something cheap, like a pack of gum, but he knew the lump in the belly of his jacket made him look guilty. His gut began to feel sick and he needed to get out of the store. He was too scared to stall any longer, and was afraid he would cry. His dad's voice echoed in his ears, "You're a wimp! Soft, just as well should have been a girl!"

Then, just like that, he knew. His game—whatever he thought it was—withered. Did he think he could prove to himself how he could be as bad as the others? Or did he hope that getting caught might keep him from ever serving like the rest of them? Cal continued to look toward the front door but his peripheral vision confirmed the guy at the counter was staring hard at him. Cal knew he was a bad liar. He wasn't like the others, the ones who lied. Yet it was too late to change course so he tried to fake it as he kept taking steps toward the door.

"Hey!" the man said. He spoke loudly, his gruff voice contradicted his balding head. A head that Cal thought looked quiet and shy with little tufts of wiry hair on the side.

Cal slowed his pace and looked down at his shoes.

"What the hell are you doing?" the man asked, louder.

Cal stopped. He looked up at the door, and then slowly turned his head to the left to acknowledge the man.

"Forgetting something?" The pitch of the man's voice rose, and Cal watched his hand move behind the counter. Maybe a phone, hopefully not a gun. The store was silent around them and he felt stuck in the moment, surrounded only by the hiss of cars driving outside on the wet street. He heard his dad's words in his ear: *Wimp. Softie. Can't do anything right*. Cal slowly shook his head and took steps toward the door.

The man yelled from behind the counter. A tear dripped onto Cal's cheek and it made him angry. *What was wrong with him?* Now he was about to fuck up this simple thing. Cal stopped and starred at the floor, unsure what to do next. He wanted to wipe the tears from his eyes, but he was afraid it would knock the lump out from under his coat.

And that was when it happened, the act he hadn't thought much about recently, until this morning with the stooped old woman who had been crying before visiting her son.

"I'll give you a minute to do what you should." The voice was suddenly gentle. Cal couldn't figure out why the voice would be soft, as if a kind man giving fatherly direction, not an angry order from someone about to call the police.

Cal turned slightly, but he knew he could not look the man directly in the eye. He was surprised to see only the man's back and he could hear the sound of papers shuffling. The man's hands moved slowly, methodically stacking papers on a shelf behind the counter as if he didn't have a care in the world. Cal hesitated with confusion. The man hadn't grabbed the phone like Cal thought he would and he wasn't sure if he felt relieved or disappointed? This monumental fork in the road that was supposed to change everything for him was ebbing away like the ocean at low tide, as if the path was being defined without Cal being the one to decide. His father's accusatory, hate-laden voice had disappeared.

Cal turned away from the door and retraced his steps back down the middle store aisle, watching his feet as he carefully took each step before stopping in front of the radios. He reached his sweaty hands under his jacket and pulled the radio out, a few tears dripped onto the floor but he felt strangely good, not bad. His hands shook as he replaced the box on the shelf, glancing back toward the counter at the man's back. Cal rubbed his fingers across both eyes, and then used the back of his hand to catch the snot from his nose. He wiped first his palms and then the back of both shaking hands on his Levi's, and sucked in a deep breath. He no longer felt like he would vomit. He strode toward the door, but stopped and glanced back toward the man before he got there, feeling he needed to say something, but not knowing what. The man was still facing the wall, so instead, Cal walked to the front door and pushed it open. The door chime celebrated the rush of marine air and blare of traffic.

It was only after this morning at the station when Calvin fully understood. All of it. There comes a time when you simply do what it is your heart instructs. You don't overthink and you may never do it again, but you do it, knowing it will all make sense one day.

Paul

IT BEGAN AS a normal enough day, as average as any other. Paul's alarm popped off at six-thirty, and a few minutes later he sat alone at the kitchen table in the house where he rented a bedroom. He artfully arranged his handful of raisins one by one over the instant oatmeal seeping in hot water before drizzling milk into his morning meal, unwavering day after day. He figured his housemate was still in bed and had come to enjoy the peacefulness of the morning, although he was glad to have a friend to catch up with in the quiet of their evenings. While so many complained about the grind of heading off to work, Paul felt fortunate that his day included time with companions he cared most about. Spirits that rarely complained or asked him to be something he wasn't; creatures that loved him unconditionally, the way he was.

He was relieved to have found work that was a mile from his home so he could continue to exist without a car, even if he no longer lived in a city boasting dozens of bus lines and trains. He believed everyone had a duty to do what they could to save the planet. That morning he was privy to a gorgeous sunrise creeping over the mountains, yellows, oranges, and reds, disappearing only as he was a block from the clinic. His scrubs peeked out from under his jacket and he didn't care how much his dress contrasted from the few folks on the street who looked more like they were about to head into the woods or onto a fishing boat.

As he entered the back door of the building, Sheila called to him from the front office. "Morning, Paul. Coffee if you want it."

He looked to her with a nod, and she smiled, she was okay that he didn't often have many words to share with her.

"It's a busy day," she said. "You might need two cups."

Paul shook his head and smiled. She knew he didn't drink coffee yet greeted him this way each morning. He entered the back room and clanked open his locker before sitting on a chair to replace his sandals with his black sneakers, placed the sandals in the locker and quietly closed it, no need for locks in the small clinic that felt like family. The vet had insisted that staff wear closed toed shoes.

Paul pushed through the next door and closed it silently behind him. "Hi guys," he said quietly. "How'd you all do last night?" He scanned the dogs, knowing them to be well cared for. He busied himself with his routine morning tasks, cleaning up urine and piles of crap first, before moving on to fill food and water bowls, making sure he took the time to greet each dog. For this morning ritual, Paul kneeled down before each animal, nestled his face in the soft fur of the outgoing dogs, carefully petting the anxious and scared ones. Paul felt the world stood still when he was in this space.

"Hey, Dora," he said as he got to the older overfed pug. He scratched behind her ears and was certain she smiled at him. "What's up for you today?" He was glad his job was mostly with the canine clients, although he had nothing against cats.

"Hey, Paul," Sierra said as she entered the room.

Paul rose after crouching in front of a dog and moved away from the cage to face her. He forced himself to look from the floor into her eyes.

"It's gonna be a tough afternoon." The vet looked at him, making sure he looked her in the eyes as if anticipating his response. "I'm sorry." She put her hand on his shoulder. Paul could feel her hesitate as if she wanted to say something more, but instead she headed back to her office.

Paul felt a dark shade was pulled over the day. In the six months since he had been working at the clinic, he knew Sierra had learned it to be important to warn him when she knew the day would include putting dogs down. The first time he had panicked in the middle of the procedure, and rather than get angry with him, she quietly called for backup and let him go home early. Now he can barely remember how he filled that day, other than walking mindlessly for hours through town. He wasn't certain he could ever fulfill that part of his job. The next day Sierra talked with him about how she made sure they only euthanized dogs when it was absolutely the last resort, or that a dog's pain level to be too high with no relief in sight. She promised him she would never do what a few other clinics were said to do: put a dog to sleep for owner convenience.

Paul would be the first to say she was the best boss he ever had, but even a good boss can't take away the eventualities of the cycle of life. He knew now it was a critical service and he didn't blame her for performing it. He sat down on the nearby stool and folded together his shaking hands. He closed his eyes and traveled to his safe space, slowing his breaths. Inhaling for five seconds, then exhaling. He said his simple prayer quietly, "All is well, all will be well." He knew this strategy wouldn't take away the heartbreaking tasks ahead of him, but he begged that it would help him make it through the day.

IT WAS LATE and Paul knew he should eat but he couldn't possibly digest food now, or maybe ever again. He always told himself afterward how dogs had short lives and he was likely to outlive each dog he ever met. Yet, knowing this did not make it easier. It was bad enough when a dog was killed in an accident or died after a sudden illness, even when they did all they could do to keep them alive. But never before had he been asked to assist Sierra to put two dogs down in one shift. He had poured comfort through locked eyes with each dog as she injected the poison. The dogs peered up at him, even after the point of where he knew they could no longer see him, with nothing but trust and love. How did they show no despair, he asked himself? The smells of the clinic, normally not noticeable to him, saturated his core: disinfectant combined with animal dander, vomit, and crap. He wasn't sure he could keep from puking. Above all else it was so quiet, other than a calm instruction from Sierra or his own instinctive comforting sounds for the dogs. Intellectually he knew it was better than them being in pain. Yet he felt he violated the trust they had in him as their heart beats slowed, breathing stopped. Trust that he could somehow make them better without it being this final act.

He didn't usually work past five in the evening, but exceptions happened on days like this. His heart was severed. On those other days like this one, he always walked the long, circuitous way home, along the riverfront trail. Often stopping here or there to look out across to Washington State, or out to sea—mostly staring without taking in what he was looking at. Most nights he'd skipped dinner all together to head to his bedroom, hoping to find a book to distract him until a new dawn appeared, bringing with it more hope than he would find during the evening.

"Paul," Sierra said as he headed toward the door. "Take care of yourself. Call me if you need." He nodded at her but couldn't fathom releasing any version of a smile.

He walked down toward the docks in town, meandering among a few boats tied up, trying to get Max and Curly off his mind. The fresh marine air brought in with it visions of the two dogs, one a slow moving golden retriever, and the other skinnier than he should be, with a bit of terrier, border collie, and who knows what else all mixed together. He imagined Max and Curly walking ahead of him on the trail, sniffing at the grasses poking up along the path. He wondered if either dog was a swimmer. Then, in his vision, Curly stopped and looked back at him before sitting patiently as if expecting the dog treat he received after each appointment. Distracted, Paul reached in his pocket automatically, found one but then tossed it aside as he let out a quiet cry.

Paul knew he needed to head home, and he returned to the Riverwalk. Max and Curly crept ahead and paused near a figure Paul could barely make out lying on the ground. Paul hesitated, only for a moment, before hustling toward them. He knelt down next to the man on the ground: he could sense the man's vitality waning. He knew to make the call, but first he offered what the man needed most in his final moments. Paul spoke quietly, and he felt Curly and Max curl up beside him. Paul offered compassion, bestowing touch and gentle words, as the immense Columbia lapped near them on its route to the ocean.

People Never Change

"WHAT DO YOU mean you can't tell me?" she asked. She waited only a split second before blurting, "I'm your wife. I'm your fucking wife!"

Calvin glanced at her, then stared down at his plate of food, as if he needed to fully concentrate on spearing a piece of roasted potato rather than listen to her, but she believed he was pissed. He just never showed it.

"Calvin, you are only a sergeant. A fucking sergeant!" She lowered her voice, knowing she shouldn't swear in front of the kids. "Not a captain, not a chief. You're not some big hero with huge secrets or privy to tremendous security risks. Get off your high horse, talk to me and join our family, would you?" Tabitha squinted while her cheeks reddened and filled with toxic air. She placed her clenched fists on the table next to her untouched plate of food. As she rose, her thigh knocked the edge of the table, causing her oldest son's juice glass to tremble. He looked at her in fear, as if spilled juice was the worst thing that might happen in that moment, thankfully naïve to how bad things got in other homes. He put his hand on his glass, as if to control something within his span. Their youngest son Ryan shirked away from the table and looked at his dad for an explanation. His mom never yelled or said bad words at his dad, not like this.

"Not now, Tabitha. Not now," Calvin said, sounding calmer than she knew he could be. The style she figured he'd learned to perfect at the jail. He gave his boys a fake smile before looking sternly back at Tabitha. "Later. I promise."

Tabitha gulped and grabbed a final lungful of air before she plunged into the abyss of the unknown, and then used it to power her voice to a volume she rarely used. "Not now? Not today, not tomorrow, not yesterday? Then when, damn it? Just keep stashing it away somewhere deep inside for never." She exploded. Those little quips she had muttered too quietly before, never sure if he'd heard them or simply ignored her. Now, she could not stop. "Like your dad and your brother? Never talking about the stuff that's killing you inside? Well here's a little secret—it's killing me too!" She looked at the kids. She knew this was a calculated, dangerous risk, and she was certain she would regret it. "Your silence is killing all of us."

The room transformed from mayhem to an eerie absence of noise. It was so quiet she could hear the clock ticking on the wall. Or was the sound her thumping heart? Until she couldn't stay quiet another minute. "I should have known when I signed that certificate you'd turn out just like your old man. You thought you could be different but no, you're becoming him!" Tabitha knew this was the worst thing she could say to Calvin.

"Mama!" Ryan cried. He reached his arms up to her, his face turned to her in fear.

Tabitha looked at her son, but her heart was numbed as she brushed her tears aside and turned back to Calvin. "Can you do the same thing to your family that you swore you never would?" Tabitha pushed back her chair as she bolted up, and it scraped against the wood floor. She hesitated, and her eyes sparked a confusing mix of fear, anger, and indecision. *Now or never.* So many times she had imagined doing this, but she had never walked out of the house in front of the kids. Yes, she had skulked out, frustrated later in the night after she had lullabied them quietly to bed and tried to get him to talk. Never before had she been triggered so much to let her guard down and expose her kids to this ugliness. Ryan was crying now, still reaching his arms to her. Joey looked questioning back and forth between his parents, willing one of them to break the horror of the scene.

There had to be a first time for everything, and Tabitha felt strangely empowered. *This is what it would take.* With clarity, suddenly she understood and felt willing to continue on without any sense of where it would take them. What was she demanding? For him to finally change, or leave? Her life would never change. Whatever boundaries Calvin and all the others like him think they can create between their day job and their family—they can't. Whatever they do and how they do it all day or night in that job, it seeps out. The anger and frustration drips, drips, drips, or in Calvin's case keeps them immune to emotion—even when they try to hide it and certainly when they refuse to talk about it. And with that, their own ambitions and hope to be different fades, day by day. Until they're a hollow shell like the ones that came before them. Except, Tabitha figured, maybe they're worse—people like Calvin— because they *promised* they'd be different. Different than all the others who can't process their lives as if their souls are silently tortured by fear, anger, trauma, and pain.

By now she had trudged across the wood floor as if in a dream, uncharacteristically ignoring the cries and startled looks from the little boys she loved more than all else, slamming the door as her exclamation mark. Strangely, she wasn't worried about Joey and Ryan. The one thing she could be assured of, so far, was Calvin would always be good to his boys. Even if he was expert at hiding what was going on for him, deep inside. He'd probably tell them something else had happened to her today, make up some big fib to avoid having it be about him. That would be his way. She loved her little boys, but why couldn't she at least have a girl who would get it? Those boys stuck together. They watched their dad and the guys that came before and said to themselves, "Yeah, we'll do it too but we'll be different." A girl, well, girls could be cops but they're smart enough not to. Most, that is. Most are smart enough to see it's not really what's good out there. "I don't want to be part of it," the smart ones said, the ones who understood they couldn't change it. Maybe someday it will be different but Tabitha doubted it.

She hadn't grabbed her coat, purse, or car keys, leaving her only escape by foot. Habit took her to the park, but she walked to the other side of the green open space, away from the playground's familiarity. It was nice out, and she had no regrets about forgetting her coat. She looked around, straining her eyes for a bench. At last she spotted one, noticing too late it to be occupied by an old woman perched on one side. As Tabitha neared, she wondered why the woman would bundle herself up to the point of pulling her knitted navy-blue sweater so tightly around her neck on such a warm evening.

She didn't look directly at the woman as she got closer, figuring she hadn't seen her as she was looking in the other direction across the park into the trees. She hoped the old woman had no interest in talking to anyone so she could simply stare off into the darkening sky and hope for a different day or to dream about what could've been. Her mom had been right, no good ever came from marrying a police officer.

What did it mean for her now: yelling so loud like that in front of the kids? She was confused and wondered if she'd have to pack a bag and show she meant business or give in, return, and pretend it was a bad night? Move on for the good of the kids, like always. Now, for the first time, she wasn't sure it was for their good but how did anyone know when *now* was the right time? Was there a sign people saw, bursting in from the universe like a game show host commanding, "Tabitha, now is your moment!" Nah. She never believed in new age crap like that. No, maybe this time it was not about the kids anymore? Her brain was spinning out of control, caught up in a mish mash of thoughts so fully consuming her the gods could shovel out-of-season buckets of snow down and it wouldn't break her from this conundrum of thoughts.

"Beautiful day, isn't it?"

Damn! Tabitha decided she would ignore the old woman.

"Beautiful day, isn't it?"

"Damn," Tabitha muttered, barely audible to someone with sharp hearing. She contemplated saying it louder, hoping it would make the woman shut up and mind her own business. Instead, as if on a roll, she erupted in unbridled frustration.

"No, it's fucking not! It is not a beautiful day!" Tabitha yelled, surprised to hear herself so angry. She challenged the woman with her stare: don't you dare talk to me! Tabitha was certain this would scare off a little old lady protected by a fuzzy cardigan.

The woman astonished Tabitha as she boldly peered back at her, eyes magnified behind thick glasses. "Well, you've got a bit of an attitude, don't you?" She said it firmly, almost nasty but not quite, like how you might reprimand a whining child.

"It is a fucking horrible day and I don't want to talk to anyone including you! Got it?" Tabitha shook, shocking herself, as if she had finally unleashed her own personal monster. A monster that had festered while restrained deep inside.

Rather than retreat, the woman gazed confidently back at her. She removed her plastic framed glasses, breathed on the lenses, and deliberately rubbed them, one at a time, with the edge of her cardigan, before slowly placing them back on her face. Tabitha knew it would only smear whatever was on the lenses and felt mean enough to point that out, but didn't. The woman then turned her body slightly so she could fully face Tabitha. Her frames were crooked, reaching above her right eyebrow and below the other.

Tabitha wanted to look at anything other than into the woman's eyes, but they bored into her. It almost made her laugh at herself to feel overpowered and frightened by this little old lady with the crooked eyeglasses.

"Well, I guess you sat in the wrong spot, didn't you?" the old woman asked much louder than before. "No nasty person is going to ruin my day today." She looked up at the sky and said as if she was addressing someone, "Just my luck, Nathan. Esther here has a real live one." She sneered.

Remarkably, Tabitha wanted to admit to this old woman, as if she were her grandmother, that she really wasn't a nasty woman. Deep down and on most days she was kind. She sighed and looked away. She wanted to tell her how she'd been pushed into silence and didn't know how to come out of it without bursting from her personal battlefield, but figured the old woman was crazy talking to the sky like that.

"Yep, I learned. I'm old you bet." The woman looked at Tabitha and smiled cynically, as she nodded. "No unhappy person is going to ruin my day, any of my days anymore." She shook her head. Then she stopped to glance around the park. "Look around you. Get your head out of your hind end. Look at the beauty of the day. If you listen quietly, the birds are singing and the roses over there blooming. Darn lucky to be alive, I say. You never know it could be your last day." She hesitated, and then dramatically took in a deep breath. "You wouldn't know, not yet. But ask me. I'm close to that last day."

Tabitha felt her defiance and anger seeping away, flowing as if sand from an hour glass. Who is this woman? All the old people she knew were lonely, sure, but they wouldn't rant on and on about beauty to some stranger. *Why in the hell did she sit down next this old crone?* Tabitha feared the old woman would start asking her questions. It's bad enough to be badgered, but if she was expected to say something in return she would certainly bolt the scene. And yet, Tabitha stayed on the bench and stared at this woman who so boldly invited her to give up, what she assumed, was a pissed off act.

Instead, the woman started talking again. Tabitha might have thought the crone was crazy but she didn't sound like the other crazies who hung out in the corners of this park, the ones she avoids when she totes Joey and Ryan to the playground. The ones Joey recently began staring at.

"Yeah, my Nathan, he was a bitter man let me tell you." Tabitha reluctantly began to pay attention to the old woman's words. The woman looked up to the sky and then back down. "Bitter man, he'd go outside—when he still could—and it'd be sunny and he'd ask, 'What good is it to be alive in this damn world?' A little dog would walk by, cute little dog, and that Nathan, he'd look like he meant to kick it, just to get it to bark so he could bitch about it. He tried his whole life to get me to be bitter, join him in his bitter club, and you know what? I almost went there, but one day, one day I said to myself, nope, Esther. No way. You be bitter all you want, but I'm not going to waste my life. And now? I'm certainly not planning to waste the time I have left to be that way."

The woman stopped talking. Tabitha felt exhausted listening to the outpouring of words, and wondered if the old woman had run out of steam. But then the woman shifted her weight on the bench, as if to prime Tabitha to know there was more.

"I must say I don't talk to much of anybody these days when I go out. But once in a while I find somebody who needs to hear a little something. A little something from me." The woman smiled, and Tabitha stared at the two gaps where teeth should be. "So maybe that's it?" Now she looked intently at Tabitha, nodded, and smiled, a sad looking smile. "Yep, maybe here I've finally found my purpose. I'll just sit here on this little bench and when somebody looks crabby, like you, I'll just speak up. Never done it before but maybe I found my calling. I have to call my daughter and say, hey, yep, you've been telling me all these years I need to do something for myself, well, here we go, I found my calling today." The woman released a gritty sounding guffaw and moved her hands in circular patterns on the rough bench seat. Then she rubbed her hands together as if she had completed a chore.

Tabitha shifted her butt on the bench, the seat of her pants felt damp. She wanted to get up and leave but felt anchored in place.

"And you know what, young woman?" the old woman prattled on. "I even ask you a question. You can listen to me go on and on about my life. You know, like I said, it's a free country. You can get up and leave, or sit and be grumpy, but I am enjoying my day. I'll sit here and listen to the birds and imagine how sweet that rose way over there probably smells, even though I don't imagine I can get myself over there to smell it at the moment. Not today, anyway. But I can sit here and remember my grouchy Nathan and how I outlived him and got to prove him wrong. I used to feel sad, sad he never got to be happy, but then I realized, you can't make somebody else happy. All of us woman think we can, but that's baloney. Parents would do a better job if they told their kids, especially their daughters, to give up on making somebody happy. All any of us can do in the end is fess up to our own feelings. Maybe the others will find happiness and maybe they won't, you never know. It's all part of that big crapshoot of life."

Tabitha was shocked at the old woman's ability to sermonize. But as abruptly as she began, she was finally quiet. She had lain her head back, resting it on the top of the bench, and was looking up at the clouds or whatever she saw above her. For a moment Tabitha had almost forgotten what she'd even been thinking about before she got to the park. It struck her, only then that whatever her own personal battle was, it felt like nothing compared to this old woman's journey. Imagine that. Being all old and wrinkled, a forgotten remnant, but finally getting to say what you wanted. And not giving a shit what anybody else thought about it. That, she thought to herself, must be freedom.

Tabitha stood up. She felt light-headed and grabbed the bench for balance. She gazed across the park in the direction the woman had been looking earlier.

"Yeah, you go on, you," the old woman said, still looking upward.

Tabitha stopped and bent to tie her shoe. Then she walked over toward the redness beckoning her. Nothing groomed or sophisticated she noticed as she neared the bush, wild. Most of the blossoms had wilted with the approach of warmer weather, rain weeks ago degraded what had been petals into a mostly unrecognizable mush. Tabitha bent down to search for a branch containing three unblemished roses hidden from the elements, avoiding any thorns as she broke it off the bush. She stared across the expanse of green to spot the blue lump perched on the end of the bench. As Tabitha neared, the old woman must have sensed her approach and opened her eyes. Tabitha saw them widen in surprise, and she bit back a smile to be the one to astonish the old woman. Stoically, Tabitha held the rose branch out toward the woman.

"Well, now, look at you," the old woman said as she reached out to receive the roses. Their fingers barely brushed, but Tabitha could discern the roughness in the old woman's skin. "Got to admit I'm a little surprised. I'm a tough one to surprise, so I guess you got me." Then she stuck her nose almost into the middle of the flower. "You know, you've really got to work for it, the smell. With these wild ones, you know. Late in the season, too. But give it a minute. You give it some time and don't expect it to be like another rose, then smell it. Then it's the best scent you've ever smelled because you didn't expect it."

Tabitha moved back to her side of the bench.

"You know it's when we think we expect something but it turns out to be different that we get so angry at life, that's another thing I learned from my Nathan." Now Tabitha waited. She figured the woman would send off a whole litany of questions now, and Tabitha would be pissed at herself for not escaping earlier, mad at herself for breaking down like usual. Instead of looking back at the old woman, Tabitha looked away, not wanting her to feel like she expected anything. She knew how this business worked.

Instead, the woman stuck her arm out, pulled the sleeve of her cardigan up to peer at a wristwatch. Faster than what any old woman with not much time left should be able to do, she rose from the bench, rubbed the back of her hips, and reached out to grab a cane Tabitha hadn't noticed before that was leaning against the bench.

"Well, I'm off. It's my time to go, young woman. Maybe I'll see you, maybe I won't," she said and walked away. "Tata," she called from a distance, as she raised her cane slightly from the ground, in farewell.

"Damn," Tabitha whispered. *Smooth.* She stood up and prepared herself for the walk she had back to her house. She took slow steps at first, dreading what she envisioned she might be returning to: kids screaming for their mama, tearful cries entering open windows of nosy, worried neighbors. Her husband angry and refusing to look at her as she entered the house with the cacophony of TV blaring and children crying. Tabitha counted her steps like she did as a child, 25, 26, 27 . . . 99, 100, 101. She looked at her feet ensconced in dark green, now threadbare, favorite sneakers with holes on one side. 150, 151 . . . she stopped. She willed herself to look up, surprised to be nearing her front cement stoop.

She felt out of breath in her efforts, not so much from the walking but the thinking. All was quiet. A few birds at a distance caught her eye. Calvin sat on the front steps. He watched her. Tabitha couldn't understand why it was all so quiet. She thought she knew what to expect. Calvin gestured to her, his forefinger slowly, quietly drawing her to him. He nodded, ever so slightly. With his other hand, the one with the wedding band, he patted the step next to him. His shoulders exuded an ever so slight shrug. Then he shared a whisper of a smile. The one she knew that said, "Please. I'm sorry."

Tabitha stopped counting her steps, nodded slightly, and went home.

The Friend

"I HAD A dream about him last night," Marie said. "I haven't thought about this kid in ages, but the dream brought him back. It was so vivid, I can't shake it." She was connecting with Taylor as they did most mornings before heading onto their daily work routine. Dripped coffee sizzled on the coffee maker burner next to her from Taylor's impatient first cup pour before it had finished its brewing cycle.

"Bad thoughts? Want me to change it up for you?" Taylor shared the look they gave her to propose sex. She shrugged the hand off her shoulder where Taylor's hand had begun to pull at her bra strap.

"No. Not like that—it was sweet."

Taylor looked disappointed.

"Just weird after all these years," she continued. "I think the last time I saw him was when I was eleven or twelve. I'm not even sure what year it was. He was an unusual kid, but we got each other."

"It's nice if it brought back good thoughts, I guess," Taylor said, pouring a second cup of coffee, this one to go. "I've got to run, but we can catch up later?"

Marie knew they were trying to be patient although seeming all too eager to leave for work.

"Yeah, sure." She looked up at Taylor's back, already heading out the door, distracted by whatever was first on the day's agenda. Marie had been trying to do her part: be less frustrated and not expect them to be able to read her mind at every moment.

She refilled her cup, adding whole milk before returning the carton to the refrigerator. The sound of the front door latch floated into the kitchen, and she hesitated to stir her coffee. With coffee cup in hand, she headed into the hall, grabbed her fleece jacket from the hook near the front door, and stepped out of the apartment. On mornings like this, she appreciated their separate outdoor entrance. She perched on the top step that led down to the sidewalk and peered below at the rumblings of her neighbors heading off to work or school or wherever they spent their weekdays. She wondered if the day would warm up or stay cool and cloudy. Gray covered the morning sky like dismal wrapping paper. Some days she wished she joined others on a journey elsewhere—a sophisticated high rise office or ornate historic building, perhaps. Most days, though, she was glad to work captive at home, a good fit for an introvert.

Fragmented scenes from her dream reformed in her mind, reminding her of school days long ago with her friend Paul. The first time she noticed him he was sitting on the concrete playground as other kids clumsily hefted junior-sized basketballs up to impossibly high rims in the distance, and yelled and chased each other round and round on a stupid play structure. The structure designed to meet ridiculous safety standards yet making it appeal only to kindergartners, no more see saws or monkey bars. She wouldn't have been caught dead joining the chase with those kids. Girls or boys, it didn't matter to her then.

She tried to think back to the time she met Paul as he sat alone on the pavement. Maybe it was because they had been stuck indoors with weeks of stormy weather and downpours that she hadn't noticed him before. That day boasted blue skies and a hint of sun and he perched cross legged, his elbows rested on his knees as he bent forward peering at the ground. When forced to join outdoor recess Marie always sat on a bench with her favorite book, even though the Duty urged her to run around and get exercise. Yes, that's what they called those nameless adults who ensured kids didn't fight, ridiculous. She knew her experience wasn't the same as all kids, but to her all the Duties and PE teachers were unkind and strict, while her favorite school mentors preferred books and libraries. Marie had finished *Eragon* earlier that day, a book her teacher didn't think was appropriate for her to read. She had forgotten to bring a new book to begin during recess, and unsure what to do with her time without reading material, she sidled carefully toward the boy. Her mom was always telling her to suck it up and stop being shy.

She was surprised the kid didn't look at her as she approached. "Hi," she began. Nothing from the boy. Now that she was closer she recognized him from her school bus. At first she thought he was younger than her because of his size. "What are you looking at?" Marie squinted to see what the boy was staring fixedly at. He had moved his legs so now they were outstretched like poorly performed splits, and he bent forward between them. His jeans were dirty from sitting on the ground. Marie walked over to sit on the ground facing him, brushing aside twigs and leaves first. She moved slowly as if she was afraid she might scare him.

The boy remained mute as he continued to stare at a bug. She thought bugs were okay, unlike a few kids in her class who squealed every time they saw a spider. Her uncle was a biologist and sometimes when her mom needed a break they hung out together, exploring parks and natural areas. When she got older her uncle told her how much he had appreciated her interest, more than his other family members. Back then when he told Marie he hoped to be a teacher she replied how he was already good at teaching kids like her. Sometimes he used too many big words, but if she asked him to explain what they meant he always did. All these years later she remembered how he taught her elaborate details about photosynthesis and meiosis, making it more interesting than the boring science teacher she later had in high school. Back then Marie couldn't wait until she was old enough to have class in labs, or at least that's what she thought when Uncle Dan told her about them.

"I don't know much about bugs," she said to the boy. He didn't look up, focusing solely on the bug. Marie didn't say anything and looked back and forth between the bug and the boy.

"This is a June bug," he said finally. His voice was quiet and deliberate. "They can eat vegetables and some people don't like them because of what they might do in your yard. But they can't hurt you." He stopped speaking, still not looking at her.

"I wonder why they are called June bugs?" Marie asked, thinking the kid wouldn't know, but now curious.

But the boy continued on, sounding more excited and as if had planned to tell her. He glanced at her with surprise, before looking back at the bug. "They are called June bugs because they come out of the soil in the beginning of summer, like now—or June sometimes. They like light, so maybe you've seen them before but didn't know it. You know, like around a light that's outside in the dark or something." The boy glanced up again at Marie's face.

"You sure know a lot about June bugs. Do you know about other bugs too?" Marie asked. She was happy talking to people who had something interesting to say, even if it was bugs, different than most of the other dumb kids in her class.

"Yes, I do. I know a lot about insects because I read about them all the time. Then I like to try to find them outside and test myself. About them."

Marie had wanted to keep talking to the boy but she couldn't think of anything more to say about the bug. "Do you have a favorite bug?" She didn't care about bugs as much as the boy, but she felt kind of bad for this kid sitting by himself with only a bug.

"Oh yes. The blue-eyed darner. It's a type of dragon fly. They're not around here much but once I saw one and I hope I can again." He held up his thumb and forefinger outstretched. "They can get this big. And their eyes are bright blue. Even bluer than my mom's." The boy looked up to meet Marie's eyes, excited.

Then the Duty had blown her whistle and Marie stood up. She watched while the boy remained on the ground, still looking down at the bug.

The Duty sauntered over. "Paul get up. Time to get back in class."

The boy who she now knew was Paul stood up, hesitating at first to bend down and pick up the bug. Without saying anything he walked toward the nearest grass. Marie had wanted to brush off his bottom so kids wouldn't tease him about the dirt all over the seat of his pants, but she didn't want to embarrass him.

The Duty raised her voice quickly, "Paul! Now!"

Marie had thought the Duty was being mean as it was obvious the boy was moving the bug to a safer place.

As he walked back toward her, Marie said, "Bye Paul."

He looked at her but didn't say anything, and she hoped he knew she liked talking with him even if it was about bugs. Even then she knew bugs were more interesting than girls and boys chasing each other and saying idiotic things.

After that when they were forced to be out on the playground at recess Marie looked for Paul. Some days she didn't see him, but she joined him on the days she did. At first, he only talked about bugs and while initially it was interesting she tried to see what else he wanted to talk about. She was challenged to try to discover what he might discuss. During their first play times together she couldn't believe how much he knew about insects and amphibians, details about colors and number of legs and even mating habits.

Soon after meeting Paul she spotted him sitting alone on the bus. She hadn't paid much attention before on those rides to and from school, busy looking out the window or reading a book, but began to notice how kids teased him or complained about having to sit next to him. Most days after a few minutes the kids grew bored and ignored him. Paul was one of the few kids who often sat alone on the bus. Marie, even then, didn't care much about what others thought of her or the names some called her—bookworm and teacher's pet. That last one she knew to be ridiculous. She thought her teachers were all dolts, teaching to what she figured was the lowest denominator. She was bored in class, and continued to place whatever book she was reading in her lap as the teacher droned on. Most teachers who noticed the book eventually ignored her, overwhelmed with loud, obnoxious kids and crowded classrooms.

One day she got on the bus and sat next to Paul. They had already talked on the playground several times—mostly with him spewing encyclopedic knowledge. This day when she sat down he glanced at her, startled.

"Hi," Marie said.

Paul nodded.

They rode in silence that day, and since Marie was sitting on the outside of the seat, when they arrived at school Paul didn't need to move out of her way, and he didn't say anything to her when she turned back to say goodbye. But from that time on they sat together on the bus and Paul began to smile at her. Kids around them continued on with what they did but Paul and Marie were now safely invisible tethered together.

MARIE'S COFFEE CUP was empty, and she felt goosebumps on her legs beneath her sweatpants. People say you remember more of the good stuff and forget the bad, but she thinks, as bad as that school with Paul was, she had always believed the next school was worse.

She opened her front door and ventured back into the kitchen, rinsed her coffee cup, and filled it with tap water. As she sipped the tepid water and looked out the window into the alley lined with two trash dumpsters and recycling bins, her thoughts floated to her mom. The dream about Paul had provoked her not only to think about their friendship, but about what happened next.

"Just let me be the way I am!" she yelled to her mom back then as a pre-teen, their relationship deteriorating. Marie hated the pedestal her mom put her on, as if she had to perform to be worthy. Her mom insisted she take difficult entrance tests for admission to a new private school, as if she needed to prove to the world how her daughter was a genius, not weird.

It wasn't until she graduated from high school that Marie understood her mom's need to show the world the accomplishment she had in her daughter, proving how successful she was to raise her daughter alone. All this confirmed to Marie that her mom loved her because she was brilliant, not because she was who she was. When Marie enrolled in this new school, boasting smart, sophisticated kids, she was sure not one of them would have sat down on the ground and studied the life of an insect like Paul. They were too busy in their intellectual dueling, a feat that killed interest for a kid like her. All she wanted was to go back to a recess where she could read her favorite books and learn about bugs from her friend. Instead she sweltered under hours of homework, studying things she cared nothing about. She was surrounded by cocky, loud kids who competed for teacher-attention and sought recommendations for elite prep schools and colleges.

Marie withdrew further and her grades tumbled as she received Cs and even a D. Her mom grounded her, unsure what else to do but not admitting it to anyone who might have been able to help. Marie snorted about how ludicrous her punishment was. Silly to ground a friendless teen who prefers the solitude of her own bedroom.

At first Marie's only authentic connection at her new school was a kind librarian who set aside titles she thought she might like. Every Friday at lunch Marie would pick up her load of books for the weekend, cram them into her backpack, and leave most of her textbooks in her locker. She looked forward to the grounded weekends as if a luxury vacation: they released her from the crap of the week. Not long after she instigated a brilliant new trigger as she swaggered to her mom and asserted no college for her. That was the beginning of the end. Her mom claimed she would throw her out of the house at eighteen if Marie hadn't figured out a decent college path so Marie began her own plan to move out the moment she was no longer a minor, circling in red ink her May birthday on her calendar.

Marie returned the empty coffee cup to the sink and stretched her arms high into the air. She checked in on the time on the microwave clock before padding over to the couch against the wall of the small adjoining living room. She pushed one of the pillows to the end and cozied herself as she curled on her side. Just for a few minutes, she thought. She felt strangely at peace. The bitterness toward her mom had been pent inside for so long and she had both refused before to dwell on it or help it unravel. And yet, in those difficult years Marie had been given the freedom to read hundreds of books, and to eventually connect with three kids who were outliers like her, including Taylor. Maybe it was time to let some of the bad melt and the bitterness fade, softened by sweet memories of the boy in her dream. She set her phone alarm for thirty minutes and wondered what she might dream next.

The Offer

ANNE?"

The masculine voice was faint but familiar. The caller's tone apologized for its intrusion. Anne knew immediately this was no bold telemarketer or someone claiming the IRS was going to put her in jail, so she did not hang up.

The call interrupted her least favorite Saturday morning chore: searching for jobs virtually from inside her Seattle studio apartment. Barely a month ago she vowed to spend part of each Saturday morning in a quest to move herself to a better place. Although not usually one to procrastinate, the moment before the phone rang she was distracted, looking away from her computer down at her bare feet, wishing she owned nail polish, even one bottle. She wouldn't care about the color— black or apple green, just to do something different. To change things up. Maybe it would pull her out of her recent funk. Her view to the world outside her brick building was stale punctuated by windows that had been painted shut, and looked down to a parking lot and street with little view of green. No Pacific Northwest tulips or rhododendron or even nuisance dandelions. If her mom knew the building was 1920s brick she'd berate Anne's apartment rental as a death trap here in the worrisome land of the Big One, expected any day or so claimed her geologist friend. Yet, she had to make more money if she ever wanted to try to swing something better. Ever since her dad's death, her job felt dead-end, stuck supporting laboratories doing research on tedious details, led by a faculty member who seemed to think they were God's gift to the world. Not mean to her, simply disinterested.

The phone rang six times before Anne answered, and she hoped the caller would give up. She received few quality phone calls these days, the only ones that weren't a threat or scam came from her two good friends and occasionally her mom. Although her dad hadn't called in a long time, his recent death made her pretend that if he was still alive maybe he would call more often.

"Yes. This is Anne," she said.

"Hi, Anne, my name is Jim. I don't know if you remember me." The voice hesitated. "I wanted to talk longer with you last month at the service, but you left before I could catch you again. I feel bad I didn't get to talk, get to know you better, but there was a lot going on. No excuses I know. Anyway, I wanted to reach out."

Anne furrowed her brows, and her bare feet alternated foot taps on the bare floor. Her toes were cold. Thoughts about nail polish dissolved into an image: *The scarecrow?* She remembered the awkward guy speaking at the memorial.

"How did you know my number?" she demanded.

"Yes. I was worried at first I didn't know how to reach you, although I imagine I could have tracked down your mother. I got your number from Marjorie. You know, at the service. She said she spoke to you a bit."

Anne hadn't been paying attention to all that he said. Her mind was preoccupied still with the struggle of reading job descriptions she was overqualified for but knew she could never land. She had closed up her browser a minute prior to receiving the call, convinced the pay was terrible for all of them anyway so why bother? Most recently she was haunted with the worry that even a dream job may never earn enough income to support herself comfortably in this city.

Clenching the phone to her ear, she rose and shuffled over to the window facing Yesler Avenue. She forced the worries aside so she could concentrate.

"I'm sorry. What are you talking about?" She knew she sounded rude. It wasn't his fault she felt crappy. "Please?"

"Your dad's memorial? I'm so very sorry too. Of course." The man sounded embarrassed, and Anne felt badly. She remembered the old woman who was kind and peculiarly interested in Anne's relationship with her dad. The woman had seemed as if she cared almost as much as Anne did that her dad was dead.

Anne walked away from the window and sunk down on the quilt on her rumpled, unmade daybed, the springs creaking as they always did. Good thing she didn't have a lover or it'd be embarrassing to make love with the noise her bed made. Although mostly all she knew about those details were things she'd seen in movies or read about.

"So, Anne. This is difficult. And, feels odd to do on the phone."

Was he a creeper? Anne wondered if she should hang up.

"You know I knew your dad, right?" the man asked.

"You did?" She recalled he had said this at the memorial but at the time she thought it was something he had to say.

She felt a stab of anger. *Why didn't she understand this then, or before he died?* After all, of Frank's three kids, she was the only one to continue to have a relationship with him. Before. Before his death. Anne closed her eyes: disjointed pieces began to come together as if solving a giant jigsaw puzzle.

"No, I didn't know. Maybe I wasn't paying attention." Don't kill the messenger. Without giving him time to respond, she whispered, "Wait. You were the one who set up the event?" Anne hesitated, biting her fingernail in a moment of silence. "I wondered who would spend the money. You know, on my dad. I don't know that he was very well liked. And he never had any extra cash. Ever."

"No, your dad did not have many friends," Jim began. "But it was more about his keeping to himself rather than not being liked. Most people simply didn't know or understand him. He had told me about you. He was proud of you for going to college. Once he told me he never forgave himself for telling you attending college was a stupid idea. Maybe another time I can tell you more about that."

Anne lay back on the bed. Tears welled up inside her closed eyes, and then stopped. She lifted her bare feet up on the quilt and rested her head on her pillow. Jim wasn't a creeper. Her pillowcase was soft and faded, barely identifying its Disney character Mulan image. She knew it was juvenile to keep these twin sheets but they comforted her. She brought her knees to her chest, feeling a familiar pain in her gut. No, now she didn't feel like crying, more like barfing. She didn't know what to say. *What did he want from her?* This was beginning to feel painful, not comforting. Although she wanted to know how he knew her dad.

Jim continued on. "I met you dad several years ago. He was feeling a bit down and out. We met at one of those AA meetings, except he never returned. But we met up here and there, sometimes sitting down on the docks together. He wasn't a mean guy and never hurt anyone that I know of. In case you wondered, because of, you know. How he died. Though he didn't always make good decisions. I'll be honest with you—I wasn't exactly courageous enough to speak to your mom. Frank, he'd told me about how he was convinced she wouldn't care if he fell off the face of the earth." He was silent. "I'm sorry. I shouldn't have said that."

The pain in Anne's gut lessened, and she lowered her legs back to the bed and turned over to lie on her back. She looked up at a cobweb in the corner of the ceiling above her. "Yeah. My dad had a skewed idea of reality." She smiled at the thought, and let out a quiet snort. It was funny if you allowed yourself to listen to Frank's old stories. Now she wished she had written some of them down.

Jim stifled a chuckle. Anne figured he thought it wasn't right, not yet, to laugh about a guy who was murdered.

"Okay," he said. Anne could hear him draw in a deep breath. "About Marjorie. The woman. She was the one who asked me to help put the event together. I'm not sure how she got my name, but Astoria is a small town and people talk. I was able to track down your mom who I assume told you about it. I did help arrange some of it, but only after Marjorie asked me to do it. She paid for everything." He paused. "Honestly, Anne. I feel bad saying this, but I can't say we would have hosted an event if she hadn't wanted to. Please remember that. I didn't get the sense your mom would have either."

It dawned on Anne, her dad might have died, and if this woman hadn't come along, whoever she was, almost nobody would have known. Maybe most didn't care much, but the abruptness of this realization stunned her. She knew her dad wasn't the greatest guy on earth by any stretch of the imagination. *But doesn't everyone deserve some kind of remembrance?* She felt more perturbed than sad, and stood up again, her body needing to be in motion. She felt prickles in her right foot as it had fallen asleep after being uncomfortably twisted. She knew she should say something, but felt confused, angry, and sad—all blended together like one might concoct in a smoothie shop for moods. She had to muster up something to say, to end this call and move on with her day. To escape her airless room.

"I don't know why you called me. But I really need to go," she said. She had an uncomfortable urge to need the toilet.

"No, wait, I'm sorry. Let me get to why I called. Here's the deal," Jim began. As he continued to talk, Anne moved back over to her table where she'd been working on her laptop. She sat down, picked up her pen, and doodled on the yellow notepad, circles and curlicues. And then a money sign. The man kept talking. She scribbled on the pad, as if a note to herself: why didn't I know this? She underlined each word and added exclamation mark after exclamation mark as she listened to Jim.

TEN MINUTES LATER Anne put her phone down. Her palms were sweaty and she wondered how long her hands had been shaking as she dashed to the bathroom. She felt like she was suffocating and had to get out of the stifling apartment, her heart was beating too fast. Even though the past few days had been chilly, she now felt she'd never gulp enough cool air, as if she was trapped in one of those weird containers that held lab mice. Anne grabbed her phone, faded denim jacket, and mace. She had promised her mom after first moving to Seattle for college that she'd never go out on her own without it, and the habit stuck these years later. She ran down the apartment stairs, too impatient for a slow elevator with a slow-moving ancient door that clanked open even on floors where nobody waited. Trancelike she headed down Yesler toward the sparkling expanse of Elliot Bay. She needed to spy water, the sight that brought her comfort when she had no other.

Jim's comment about Marjorie jarred her. "Her son had been accused of killing your dad." How could that be? When she learned somebody had killed her dad she couldn't imagine who would do it. Deep down she didn't even believe it and kept expecting to learn the medical examiner had screwed up, mixed his body up with somebody. That he had instead died because of a run-of-the-mill heart attack, boring death for an average life. Because, after all, her dad was basically a lot like any other Joe out there. Sometimes pathetic, but he never did anything exciting or unique enough to die tragically. She felt that way more as she had gotten older and had begun to understand how short lifetimes were: nobody had days to waste doing nothing. Yet it troubled her that as much as he talked, he never would have hurt anyone. Even in his heaviest drinking years. Instead, it was as if Frank was filled up with frustration and there was a rubber stopper keeping it from releasing, kind of like a test tube in her high school science lab. Anne had refused to listen to her mom when she insisted on reading the police report to her over the phone, only getting her to stop by threatening to hang up. But now, to learn not only that someone was suspected of killing *him,* but to have hugged the killer's mother?

Anne's heart beat wildly, and her face felt hot. She wondered if someone her age could have a heart attack? She felt as though she was reenacting the moments immediately after she learned about her dad's death. Knowing about Marjorie and her son—it made the incident concrete. And this guy's mom wanted to make it up to her? Nobody could make something like this okay again. What was the old woman thinking: pay her off? Was that why she had been sucking up to her, at the service?

Anne reluctantly allowed her memory of the comfort of the hug, its softness, and the smell of lavender conquer her anger. Marjorie had fully embraced her, even when her own mother could barely manage a stiff one-armed hug. No, Anne couldn't feel angry. Nothing would bring her dad back. Maybe he was finally at peace? But it all felt complicated. In addition to accepting that her dad had died, she thought more about how he never felt satisfied while living—unless maybe his joy was in the spinning of stories? The not knowing but the imagining. As far as she knew Frank never found the treasures he sought, and few of the promises he made to her came true. Those fantasies he had chased from as far back as she remembered. Was that it? He told stories, and it mattered less to him if they ever came to fruition.

Startled, she felt guilty to be so late to understand her dad's true nature. And now to learn she might benefit from his death. How could any child feel okay about that? She was numb after hanging up the phone with Jim, likely incoherent by the end of the conversation and she doubted to have said anything meaningful. Anne struggled to say she'd think about it, spitting out the words as she hung up the phone. When she finally ended the call, she felt an entire day had elapsed.

Now, as if having sleepwalked, she had trudged twenty blocks downhill to the edge of the Elliot Bay pathway. It was not yet noon on a weekend, and although she nudged the mace buried deep in her pocket, she felt safe and comfortable in this place. More comfortable here than in the busy lit commercial streets of downtown next to Nordstroms or Starbucks, or her stuffy, cramped apartment. She stopped and rested her elbows on the handrail at a viewpoint. Two ferries passed as they continued their voyage, one back to port in Seattle and the other probably off to Victoria or another island, she wasn't sure. She heard a boat blast its warning as it passed the other, but the sound was soon lost in the rumbling of traffic and squawks of gulls. The smell of the fishy marine air calmed her heart into beating its normal rhythm.

After a few minutes, Anne crossed her arms, pulling the warmth of her body deep into her core. She felt something rustle in the top front jacket pocket and pulled out the envelope she had forgotten about. She had received it from her dad in the mail just a few days after his death. Then it had felt like a monstrous joke. Never before had he mailed her a twenty-dollar bill. She eyed her name and address scratched in his willowy writing on the envelope's front, pulled out the flattened bill, before folding it to hold tightly in her hand. She replaced the envelope to her pocket, looked out to the water again, and smiled. *Her treasure.* Anne giggled.

Toward the end of the call with Jim, he had asked her what she wanted more than anything else. Anne couldn't remember the last time someone had asked her that question. Maybe when she graduated college? Back then it seemed perfunctory, as if it's what you asked every graduate on the verge of entering the real world. Then, it had frustrated her, as if she could share her real dreams and believe that in the world of today she'd ever be able to hope to reach them. Sure, maybe if rich people around you hosted you in the door, but not kids like her. They liked to make you feel like you could but she knew better. No, the last person who authentically asked her what she wanted was Mr. Anderson back in high school. He was the guy that genuinely cared about her answer. And although he did say she could do anything she set out to do, his message was different. She knew none of it would be easy, no golden paved roads for her. But now, these years later to be asked what she wanted? She was confused but weirdly excited. Did this mean she was glad her father was murdered so she could do something she wanted to do?

Anne continued walking, passing the usual people looking for handouts. She once was startled by those on the streets begging, and would avoid walking by them if she didn't have a few coins to drop into whatever they'd put out, hats or bowls or outstretched hands. Soon she joined the ranks of those passing by who became hardened to it, but unlike some, she looked each one in the eye and forced a weak smile as she shook her head. She knew she couldn't fix all that and it made her sad all over again. But today instead of doing what she did on autopilot, she opened her hand and dropped the crumpled bill into the hat held by an older man, disheveled in his fleece jacket and drooping jeans. The man's eyes opened in surprise, and he smiled at her.

"God bless," he said.

Anne smiled.

She took another deep breath and forced herself to identify the salt and rot all mixed together in the air she inhaled. The sky looked like it might rain soon, and although she didn't care if she got wet or was out without a raincoat, she was ready to get back. Her soul was saturated with freshness, and its bottled staleness had dissipated. She looked out over the water, clouds and mist blocking a noonday sun. She remembered the stories about buried treasures, gifts promised. She imagined Frank's grin when they once rented a metal detector up by the Column. She wondered what he might think about this ultimate treasure, his final story. Then she turned around and headed home to call Jim to accept the offer.

A Mother's Heart

WHAT DOES A mother do? The first morning, the question circled repeatedly in Marjorie's brain, like wet clothing tumbling in a dryer. It appeared vaguely at first, a fleeting sensation she could not decipher like a cloud filtering out sunshine, growing until it encroached into each moment's thoughts, yet somehow remaining undefined. It left her feeling bleak and hopeless. Until later that night the sensation morphed into what it was, this single question.

The next day the question gave birth to another. *What should a mother do?* No matter how she answered the questions she knew, if not for her, there would be no Paul and no accusation. Marjorie was left with the terrifying fear that if she had no son this other man might still be alive. For days she remained uncertain: was Paul innocent or guilty?

When finally, the accusation against Paul was dropped, but without a clear resolution, she could not escape her question, uncertainty persisting as if dropped bread crumbs. Would her doubts degrade over time in the way crumbs decompose in a forest? Once the idea was planted, how could a parent ever cease wondering if their own child took another man's life? A man who was a father.

Now, days after the question first gyrated in her brain she continued to speculate about what she should do next even as her thoughts jerked her to reminisce of early days with Paul. Marjorie walked through the quiet streets of this unfamiliar town, careful to step over twigs and leaves ripped from pines and firs whipped to the sidewalk during the last storm. She wanted to climb the steeper streets up to the quiet, historic neighborhoods to locate the tourist spot the dog-eared brochure in her cottage mentioned, the Astoria Column. Yet the hill climb was daunting to her now, and she lacked the initiative to return to her car in search of it.

She was staying a few miles away in a trendy tourist town, sleeping alone in a simple cottage. A cottage with a tiny kitchen equipped with a microwave, electric tea kettle, and sink, mostly rented out by the week. She first reserved it for three days, not imagining she would soon decide to stay a full week. And then, earlier today she told the motel manager she might want to stay on a second week, craving her own comfortable bed but too tired to summon up energy to return home. Driving three hours through winding mountains, even in day light, was no easy feat anymore.

Marjorie was torn by her desire to figure out what to do next or her wish to simply return to her life of before, one sated with predictable routine. When the police call came, she numbly pulled together a suitcase, asked her neighbor to feed her cat, and tried to gather her wits. The neighbor begged her not to go.

"Marjorie, you're too old for this. Let someone else help Paul," Jill pleaded with her. "You barely drive to the grocery store these days," she said quietly, probably not wanting to sound like the pack of people insistent on taking car keys away from old folks.

Marjorie ignored the comments and thanked Jill for taking care of Tinkerbell, before handing over her spare house key and returning home. Let someone else help Paul? There was nobody besides her to help Paul.

Now she wondered if it had been a mistake to encourage Paul to move away to this distant town? Maybe it was too soon after finishing his schooling. She was swayed by his intelligence, and her own naivety, operating as his mother even though she was old enough to be the grandmother. He was a smart kid and why shouldn't he move out like any other grown up kid? As normal as any other she asserted, as if in conversation with another part of herself. Crazy to refer to any kid as normal, all of them exhibiting unique gifts, traits, and impairments: about this Marjorie was certain. Oh, but what a horrible thing to be exactly like everyone else, she had always said. "Life would be boring if everyone was the same," she told Paul over and over. Paul was kind and sensitive in a way most people didn't understand or appreciate. But was he a killer?

Marjorie wasn't one to be able to walk miles at a stretch anymore, and she needed to rest. She didn't feel like stopping in a shop or café, and she was relieved when she spotted the public library across the street.

"Perfect," she whispered, surprised to have worked up a sweat in the chilly air. "Quiet and cool."

She pulled the handle of the glass door open and stepped into the main room of the small library, nothing like the three floors and dozens of rooms offered by her county library back home. A librarian looked up at her from across the gray carpeted room, offered a glimpse of a smile, and looked back down at her paperwork. The room felt more like a small school library, reference materials shelved against one wall and a few tables offering space to work while sitting at uncomfortable-looking chairs. Marjorie shuffled to a padded arm chair near a wall and collapsed into it, immediately regretting not to have taken a book from a shelf first. Yet, it felt good to sit. She was relieved not to see anyone paying attention to her, and she sighed as she recognized how silly she was to imagine she could set off on a lengthy walk like she might have ten years before.

Her thoughts returned to Paul. Out of nowhere floated the memory of a time he accidentally stepped on a bug on the sidewalk.

"Tell it to move, Mama!" six-year-old Paul cried out.

Back then Marjorie had considered lying to him and telling him the bug was only napping. Instead, she softened the truth. "It's okay, honey. It was just an accident. He's only a little bug." She remembered having reached down to grab Paul's hand so they could continue to walk home.

"No, Mama!" he had cried, this boy of hers. "Make it move. Make it be okay," he insisted, raising his voice.

He dropped down to the ground where he sat cross-legged as if to command a vigil to bring the bug back to life.

"C'mon, Mama, help me," he ordered her.

At that time, Marjorie was struggling to learn how best to handle Paul's difficult moments, adjusting her strategies to match each new developmental stage. A neighbor had approached them then on the sidewalk, an initial nod of understanding morphed into his embarrassed smile as their eyes met, before he sped up to pass the two of them. Paul's yells at the bug to come back to life progressed into tears and heavy sobbing. She repeatedly attempted to soothe him without success, until he collapsed prone on the sidewalk fully exhausted. He was too big for her to carry and even her promise of an ice cream cone failed to get him to move. Now, in the quiet and anonymity of this small-town library, she couldn't remember how she finally got him to stand up and make his way home.

It was after the dead bug outburst that she took his sensitivities more seriously, accepting he might not simply grow out of them. Paul felt things deeply that most kids shrugged off. Many things bothered him, loud noises or, like the bug, something that might be in pain. Marjorie began interpreting silent questions others shared through disapproving glances, and her mantra became, "He's sensitive. My boy, he cares a lot." She was Paul's biggest champion, reconfirming to him whenever she could that, yes, it is okay to feel things deeply. To care deeply. Even to this day, sitting alone in the library miles from her home, she knew this was true.

And that was why the contradiction of the accusation stunned and overwhelmed her. Who would believe her son to care about others if they read the news article carelessly tossed into the Astorian the day after, with his name listed as a person of interest? A detail like that, true or false, might haunt someone to the end of their days. Perpetuating this newest question of hers: what does it do to the mother? True, false, half-true, half-false. What does any of it mean now, now that the question has been planted? She believed deep in her heart Paul didn't kill this man. He couldn't have. Yet, if others believed it, the nagging question resides within her: Had she done everything a mother should do? She was certain she had showered her love only to him, taking on the excess burden of worry and fear she believed he couldn't handle. She never asked for help, not even when others offered. Not even when others wondered. She protected him by being there at every moment of need. Until she wasn't.

Marjorie had few friends who understood that life wasn't always a good match for Paul. Some people wanted to name why he was this way, but most of what they said did not fit her son. Besides, why do they think they need a name for everything? He was just a boy, a special boy made by God to be on this earth. A boy who never did understand why a bug might get stepped on needlessly. "Why?" he would ask, over and over. Why didn't everyone care about all creatures like he did, he wanted to know. The creatures he cared for now, or did at least before all this, earning enough to pay part of his way. During his childhood she never allowed him to get a pet, telling him instead her demanding work hours made it impossible to be a good pet owner. In her heart she knew it was because all pets die, maybe sooner than later. Death of a loved pet would be something she could never allow for Paul. But now she wonders if it would have helped her son if back then his favorite dog or cat or hamster had died?

Maybe that's where she made her gravest motherhood error. She tried hard to shield him from horror, death, and pain. Yet life was full of it: pain, rejection, hurt, death. *Just what was she thinking? Stupid!* She flicked her fingers out as if expressing her ignorance to a companion. Marjorie looked down at her sturdy walking shoes, distracted by the feeling of sand inside her socks. She shook her head. Maybe those smart people with all those long words might have told her that instead of her thinking all Paul needed was love. Even with all the love she doled out she had failed—had she incorrectly calculated the prescription to help Paul safely make it through this world without her?

Marjorie reached into her purse and pulled out a tissue, first staring at its faint flower pattern before dabbing her eyes. She glanced at the desk, hoping the clerk couldn't see she had begun to cry. She was tired but knew she should return to the cottage before dark, so she pulled the strap of her handbag to her shoulder and heaved herself out of the chair by forcefully pushing her hands on its arm rests. The chair scraped the floor and a man she hadn't seen before, sitting nearby with a thick reference book on his lap, looked over at her. Marjorie returned a quick nod and walked to the door. On a normal day, she would have thanked the librarian, but this was no normal day. As she took her first steps outdoors she questioned if she could make it back to her car. The cooler air disoriented her at first but she was relieved to remember the direction she needed to walk, and trudged slowly. Maybe it was finally time to get a cane. She sighed.

A school bus passed her, reminding her of the particularly bright and hopeful time when Paul was in elementary school. Marjorie had thought then it might be the one thing to change everything. She subscribed to parenting magazines in those days where columnists advised worried parents about the importance of kids having at least one good friend. *One buddy who laughs with you, but not at you.* Paul had a good friend for a while. She was named Marie and wore her dark hair in a long braid. "Her hair goes all the way to the bottom of her bottom!" Paul had exclaimed one day, and then he had giggled. She thought his giggles had dried up years earlier.

Marjorie had met Marie's mother once during a rare play date. This mother was reserved, and Marjorie sensed she didn't like the two kids to play together. Marie's mother, in a never repeated moment of confidence, told her that she braided Marie's hair each Monday morning, leaving it alone until the following Monday morning. It was a mother-daughter pact they had made, keeping her from touching her sensitive daughter's hair the other six days of the week. When Marjorie learned this, she thought they might have something in common as parents, but the woman never initiated another conversation.

Paul hadn't had a non-imaginary friend before Marie, and he was new to the rules of friendship. Somehow the two kids figured out how to do it. Some nights after a few months into their school-based friendship, Marjorie told her sister how relieved she felt for her son to have this Marie. She didn't admit to her sister or anyone else how much she hoped this would be the start of life being kinder to Paul.

Then, just like *that* it was gone. Marie and her family abruptly moved away, and Paul didn't see her at school or on the bus. Marjorie was unsuccessful in learning any details about her whereabouts, and they never heard from Marie or her mother again. Once again—Paul was alone. No longer did he have a friend to laugh with. Instead he was left with kids who laughed at him.

Soon after Paul declared he no longer wanted to attend school. Before knowing Marie he had never complained about school. When Marie had been in his life Paul glimmered with joy as he reported out at dinner what he had done during the day. When Marjorie waited with him at the bus stop in the morning he was often excited as he would tell her, "Today I will be with my friend." Marjorie knew they shared secret jokes. She tried to get Paul to tell her what they talked about or did together, but a new level of maturity and privacy entered with the friendship. Paul wasn't rude about it, instead offering what she thought to be a prematurely adolescent remark, "You wouldn't understand."

After Marie moved, instead of stoically heading to the school bus like he had in the days before Marie, or skipping ahead of his mom when they were friends, he would shake his head and beg to stay home. Worse were the days when he would cry and retreat to his bed, something he hadn't done in years. Marjorie tried to cheer Paul up, until, exhausted, she stopped trying. She needed to go to work but instead used precious vacation leave until she found another school for Paul. It had seemed better suited for him and he bonded one year with a teacher who seemed extra special to him. A teacher, she remembered thinking at the time, that might make all the difference. And yet, Paul never again loved school the way he had when Marie was his friend.

Marjorie stopped walking. She had been consumed by memories and had no idea where her car was parked. Her heartbeat quickened: was she lost? She was thankful the sun was still high enough in the sky so she could find her car and make it back to the cottage. She looked back the way she had walked and was relieved to spot her blue Honda half a block back. *I need to be more careful.*

Marjorie walked back to her car and pulled the keys from the outside pocket of her bag. She unlocked the door and groaned with relief as she sat on the warmed car seat, still chilled from sitting so long in the library. She was ready for a nap or an early bedtime, but knew she must concentrate on driving to arrive safely back at the cottage. All the reminiscing led her to another question in the swirling sea of questions. Perhaps, after Marie, was when she should have done something. After he lost his friend and broke his heart. She has no idea what it was she might have done, for no school counselor or teacher ever warned her that Paul was headed on some bad path. None of them knew Paul like she did, though. She was the one who dedicated her life to make each moment better, falsely believing he would grow out of it, all the while Paul must have learned to pretend everything was okay. And now, was it too late?

Marjorie started her ignition, set her blinker even though the only cars on the street were parked, and pulled onto the road. She carefully focused to get her car headed south on Highway 101. She stopped at a red light.

"It's never too late," she told herself.

Yes, there was still time as long as her ticker still beat. She would have the chat, the one she should have had with her son long ago. No matter where Paul was, she would find a way to begin the conversation, however difficult to find the words or admit the errors of her ways. Although the light turned green, Marjorie kept her foot on the brake and peered up the steep hill to her left. A column climbed up toward the clouds, rising above rooftops and trees. A car behind her honked, and Marjorie abruptly took her foot off the brake and motored through the light. Although she knew she could not predict the future, she felt relieved to identify the path ahead.

A Wave's Nudge

THE BEACH HAD appeared endless as she began walking. Marjorie turned and stopped, her back to the headwind. She gazed southward, knolls of dune grass peaked above gray sand, blades waving with the wind, headlands in the distance. Her return walk would be easier if she first walked against the wind. She knew she would thank herself later. She squinted through darkened glasses she didn't need today but wore them anyway for the prescription they offered. She had forgotten to tuck her regular glasses into her purse and worried for a moment that she may have left them somewhere. Each day she noticed her vision less acute than before, even with correction.

Far north of her, barely visible through the moisture laden clouds was the edge of what she knew to be a lighthouse. She tried to picture how the structure might be perched on a cliff overlooking the ocean, waves crashing on the rocks down below, and the narrow jetty made of rock and concrete she believed to be nearby. If she didn't know it was there, though, she'd never be able to decipher its image through the billowing clouds. She winced down at her feet but gave a barely noticeable shrug. She knew already it had been a mistake to leave her sturdy tennis shoes at the trail head, but walking in the wet sand made her feel younger than she was, even though her arthritic toes already complained about walking barefoot. She'd need a double dose of Tylenol in the morning. She imagined hearing the wet sand squeaking between her toes, but knew any sound coming from her feet was blocked by the pounding surf.

The blurred blob she had first seen at the edge of the water became two distinct figures, one towering over the other. While she had hoped for complete solitude during her beach walk, she smiled. Beaches were meant for children. Children and seagulls. She heard squeals, guttural but high pitched, as the foamy waves encroached on the nearby couple. Closer still she noted the waves were losing energy, softening into ripples as they surrounded the blobs, figures identifiable now to be a small boy and man standing in a few inches of water. The gentle waves no longer carried the white-capped energy of those further offshore, and she walked closer to the tideline, avoiding a piece of kelp and a slimy pile of jellyfish and seaweed. The child tottered back and forth, first on one foot, then the other, back and forth, flinging wet sand onto his baggy shorts and bare chest each time he stomped his foot into the water. His shorts' profile outlined a bundle of diaper inside. Down again into the water a foot would disappear, coming out again as if to the rhythm of a drum beat. Marjorie couldn't tell if he teetered because he was only learning to walk, or if the excitement of the incoming waves and his exuberance left him off balance.

"He reminds me of someone I once knew," Marjorie said, near enough now, she thought, to be heard. Her words were caught in the roar of the ocean and grunts of gulls.

"This is his first time in the ocean," the man replied.

Marjorie felt comforted to have been heard.

"He was here as a baby, but I doubt he remembers any of that, and of course he couldn't run around like now." The man glanced up at her. "Freedom. I think he is sensing a new freedom for the first time." He wore only a tee shirt with his jeans, a day pack crammed full on his back, probably discarded sweatshirts and coats.

You'd think he thought it was summer, Marjorie thought as she stifled a shiver.

The man was near enough to catch the boy if he lost his balance, but far enough to allow the little guy to imagine he was independent in his quest to explore. She knew all about that and the accompanying delicacy of toeing the line, a skill she never mastered. Now understanding that more than ever. The man had rolled up his jeans, but she noticed the bottom two inches above the faded denim hem were wet. She would like to have a grandson like this, she mused. She chided herself: a silly thought when she was old enough to be a grandmother to her own son.

"We came every summer," Marjorie said. "For at least ten years, I imagine. Until . . ."

The man kept his eyes on the boy, and she wasn't sure he heard her. He glanced at her. She didn't believe he wasn't being rude, simply unwilling to take his eyes fully off the boy. The man glanced at her again and released a wide smile, exposing white, perfect teeth. Marjorie stayed silent as her mind crept down the rabbit hole as it did so often in these past few years, not surprising with this beach visit. Even at her age, she remembered the last summer with her boy's father as much as the first one. The last summer of life as they knew it. Still beautiful, she stubbornly reminded herself, insisting that she not forget the joy of those earliest days.

Marjorie smiled and suddenly stomped her feet, carefully. The wet sand was peppered with ridges, micro hills, and valleys pounded into place by water finding its way back to the ocean. She held her arms out to balance herself as she mimicked the boy, forcing herself to be in the moment. She blinked to bring her bearings back to this day at the ocean and not rehash those times when the nightmares, anguish, and heartache began. Each year worsened ever so slightly with each new day she forgot what it was like when it had been better.

"No," she said quietly, shaking her head. Her word too soft to compete with the roar of the waves.

Marjorie looked down at the boy and then moved closer, bending down, not too close to frighten him but near enough to see his reddened cheeks and how his long eye lashes were clumped together with salt water. She tried to hide the soft groan released as she felt the achiness in her knees caused by crouching. Boldly now, she peered closer at his face, and then back to where the energetic waves crash in the surf, trying to imagine what it would be like to see them for the first time. All of it fresh and clean and good. Without memories of bad in the past, not in this moment.

The little boy kept marching, stomping first one foot, then the other, shrieking with each splash that rose up and soaked his shorts, diapers, and t-shirt. Marjorie was surprised to see the edges of wet cloth diapers dangle down his leg. He stomped his right foot so hard that water splashed onto her leg. She had rolled up her pants, but salt water wetted the fabric. The little boy's eyes grew large with worry, and Marjorie wondered if he only now noticed her. His smile melted and his eyes twisted in concern as he turned to look up at his dad, and then quickly back at her.

Marjorie knew he was wondering if he done a bad thing, splashing her. At this, she laughed, releasing a bellyful of joy, unleashing a tightly woven ball of pent up sadness and pain expelled as exiting a burst balloon. All this let loose by a simple splash of water. The little boy's eyes widened at her noisy laugh, and he giggled. He turned to eye his father to see if he too shared this private joke. The father smiled back. And then he chuckled.

Marjorie smiled, first at the boy, and then back at the man. Without thinking, she took a careful step closer to the boy before kicking at the water, splashing him below his hips. The little boy looked at her in surprise. Then he too released a belly laugh. Laughing, he fiercely stomped up and down before pulling one hand away from his father to reach down into the water and splash her. The father held the boy's other hand firmly, but used his free hand now to splash the little boy. The boy looked at his father, and excitedly back at Marjorie: the father carefully splashed her.

The little boy staggered and fell down on his bottom into the water, the soft rippled water almost covering his hips. He looked at his father in surprise, unsure whether to cry or laugh. The father grabbed the boy by his arm pits until he noticed Marjorie shake her head, and he stopped. Marjorie tucked her handbag higher around her shoulder, raised both arms to balance herself and carefully lowered her no longer agile body down in the water next to the boy. Then she laughed.

The boy's eyes and mouth opened wide and he glanced at his father, then looked back at her. And then he laughed and lifted his chubby arms up toward his dad. "Daddy. Come. Daddy now. Come," he said as he tried to pull his daddy to the ocean floor. His dad looked around him on the beach, shook his head, and smiled.

"Better just join them," he muttered with a smile before he plopped down. Then he too laughed.

Marjorie could not contain her belly laughs, howling until tears came, finally subsiding into giggles and a snort. Relieved and refreshed by this moment of laughter.

The roar of the ocean faded and the waves continued to retreat from the high tide mark. The little boy bobbed his legs back and forth until the waves stopped spilling over him, leaving his feet and legs crusted with wet sand. The excitement over, the little boy maneuvered himself to a standing position, leveraging himself against his father's body, before pulling at the man's hand. The man stood up, and the little boy looked at the old woman, puzzled. He reached out his small hand to her.

"I'm a big old woman, little guy." She laughed. "It's going to take way more than little you to get this one up."

He smiled at her as if to tell her he didn't believe her. She tried but could not get her feet positioned beneath her. "I should have done all that yoga," she muttered.

The man gently grabbed her other arm, the little boy reached out for her leg but his sandy fingers slipped. He looked up at the pair as they towered above him, and brought his hands together, celebrating, as his father helped Marjorie to her feet.

While Marjorie balanced herself carefully, the little boy dropped his hand from her leg to reach her other hand creating an intimate circle between the trio, hands and legs and feet speckled with Pacific Ocean sand. The little boy dropped his hand and ran back toward the retreating waves.

"More!" he said.

The father dropped Marjorie's hand and ran after his son. Marjorie stood and smiled at their backs. The man grabbed his son's hand, and then turned away from the waves to look back at her. She waved. The man picked up the boy and pointed toward her and the boy waved his small hand. Marjorie hesitated before blowing off a kiss.

Her knees were stiff, as usual the right one worse than the left. Her right ankle throbbed as she turned, her back now to the head wind. The draft of air pumped up her confidence to endure the trek to the trail where she entered the beach, even as her knees creaked and ankle ached. A sweet bliss enveloped her, softening her joint pain and reviving her wounded heart.

She walked along the beach, plodding from wet sand to the heavy dry sand that seemed to grab her feet like quicksand, and aimed for the trail marker pointing to her rented lodging. The cheapest room she could find nearest the beach. This new feeling continued to seep in, replacing her sourness. Her right ankle pain increased, yet her body felt lighter, filled with a knowingness lighter than helium. She had spent her time, she and her son, and it had been good. But it was over. That time was gone, and he was grown. He was a grown man. And somehow, for the first time, that gave her comfort, great comfort.

A Drop of Water

"JACK MET A new friend at the beach today," Sam said to his wife at dinner.

The kitchen table tipped slightly as he rested his elbows on its edge, and he scolded himself for not having yet repaired its wobbly leg. He reached down to the floor to pick up a cracker Jack dropped from the highchair tray, before looking back at Beth. She intently cut her salad into smaller pieces. He waited. Was she lost again in her thoughts?

"Really," Beth said, finally, without inflection.

Sam concentrated on the food on Jack's tray and ignored Beth's disinterest.

"Yes, really," he replied, antagonized by what sounded like a rotten mood even though he'd tried to give her a day to herself. His wiser inner voice told him to drop it. He was still thinking about how the connection with the woman earlier had made him feel.

"Well, tell me. The least you can do if you bring it up is to tell me about it." Beth peeked up from her plate and sent Sam the "I mean business look," the one where she clenches her lips tightly together and raises her right eyebrow. Her cute left dimple always shows which undercuts the look's meaning, even though he'd never tell her.

"You don't have to be snappy," Sam said. He hesitated. "I just thought it was fun and you'd like to know." He stood up and grabbed his glass, eyed Beth's still full drink, and walked over to the faucet. He turned the tap on, waiting for it to run cold before refilling the tumbler, wishing they had a window to peer out of from the sink like most kitchens. The tile grout in the backsplash was growing black mold. He sighed.

"I'm sorry. Tell me. Really." Beth did not sound sorry.

Sam returned to the table, set his glass down and shrugged. He reached to the floor to pick up the spoon Jack had thrown.

"Just a second," he added, grabbing a paper towel from the table, bending down and first encircling and then picking up the mashed green clump from the linoleum and set the wad next to him on the table.

He sat back down, looked at Jack and smiled, deciding to give Beth the benefit of the doubt.

"There was this old woman who struck up a conversation with him." Sam hesitated. "Well, not really a conversation. You know." He couldn't help but smile at Beth about this boy they shared. "She started splashing him."

Beth let out a mama bear snort. "Why? What an awful thing to do to a little kid."

"No, no, not like that. I'm not explaining it very well." Sam sighed and regretted he hadn't left the unadulterated memory alone. He should have just written it down so he might share it with Jack someday but it felt too late now to memorialize private thoughts. "She did it for fun, like a game. You know, just a tiny splash because—you know how Jack is when he gets his feet in water? Multiply that by a hundred as to how much he loved the waves today." Sam couldn't stop himself from sharing the joyous encounter he and Jack had shared at the beach. "The old lady had been watching him and simply splashed him."

"What?" Beth asked. "This just sounds weird. Was something wrong with her?"

"Maybe you had to be there," Sam said, deflated. His mood had been good earlier, but now he was beginning to feel as if the incident hadn't happened. "Eventually we were all sitting in the water, but it doesn't seem the same trying to describe it now. It was cool. Trust me. There was something about her."

"What?" Beth asked. She gave him that warily accusatory look, as if he was lying or doing something wrong. Early in their relationship he would tease her that it made him imagine a sexy Minnie Mouse, personally suffering but wanting more than anything to understand the issue. He'd never tell her this, but more recently she reminded him of a modern-day Maleficent.

"Are you jealous?" he asked. After saying it, he felt badly. He had been trying to give her the break of a relaxing day alone, but now it was hard once again. He knew she was struggling balancing being a mom and work and who knew what else. He inhaled deeply, slowly releasing his breath, as he chided himself not to stir anything up. He put his hand on top of hers, and looked into Beth's eyes. Beth issued her other look, the one to remind him she didn't fully believe the words of her handsome partner.

"The lady was old. Like a billion years. It's not what you seem to jump to all the time." Sam pulled his hand away.

Jack picked up a cracker from his tray and threw it down to the floor, looking first at Beth and then back at Sam with his impish smile.

"Your turn," Sam said, smiling at their smart son who had already learned how to interrupt their loud words.

"Alright," Beth said, with a quiet laugh. She shook her head, grabbed the cracker, and placed it on the table, out of Jack's reach. "You smart little guy," she told Jack, kissing his ear and holding his little hand.

"It's hard to explain," Sam continued, wanting her to understand. "She said Jack reminded her of her son when he was little. That's all she said and it would have been nothing, but she seemed emotionally mixed up as she watched Jack so joyfully, but sad too." He looked at his wife and son and smiled. "You would have liked seeing it."

Sam stood up and took the few barefooted steps to the kitchen counter. He cut a small piece of pizza from the remaining pie in the box on the counter, and sat down again.

"More," Jack said.

Sam put a piece of his leftover crust on the highchair tray, and Jack grabbed it with his fist and jammed it into his mouth, pulled it out again, and then looked between Sam and Beth with his mostly toothless grin.

"Does she live around here?" Beth asked, as if only now she was a bit curious.

"I don't know. Truthfully, we didn't talk much. It was mostly between Jack and her, I think." Sam moved Jack's sippy cup closer to him. "What do you think, Jack, buddy? Did you make a new friend today?"

Jack's cheeks were reddened and Sam hoped he didn't get too much sun. Jack jabbered his talk, his mouth full of gummy crust pieces, reddish slobber leaking from the sides of his mouth, and thumped his hand on the tray.

"Okay, okay, enough buddy. Time for your bath." Sam unhooked the high chair tray and set it on the table. "I will take him if you clean up?"

"Sure. That's the deal, I guess—you *made* dinner," she replied. He wasn't sure if her response was meant to be snarky, but willed himself to give her the benefit of the doubt.

LATER THAT NIGHT after Beth had picked up the kitchen, he had bathed Jack, and they both put him to bed, Sam thumbed through the contacts on his phone. They were in the living room, Beth stretched out on the leather couch with a book rested face down on her stomach, her head propped up on a pillow and her eyes closed.

"What was the name of that woman you used to work with in the shop?" Sam asked. "You know, the one that had the loud mother she always apologized about but who was kind of a hoot? Remember? We learned last year that she had died? I mean her mother had?" His hair was wet and he sat in an upright chair in his frumpy navy sweat pants and stretched out orange Oregon State University tee shirt.

Beth's eyes remained closed. He wondered if she was asleep, still fully clothed.

"Oh, do you mean my friend—well, she wasn't close mostly—but Sarah?" Beth asked sleepily, not opening her eyes.

"Yeah, her, I think," Sam said. "You know, long dark brown hair, kind of scrawny? Uh, sorry, thin? Swore a lot?" He hesitated. "Did you ever call her after her mom died? To give your condolences, or whatever it is we're supposed to do when people die?"

"No, I don't know. It didn't seem like I needed to. We weren't *that* close. Not really. It's not like we did things together outside of work." Beth opened her eyes and lifted up her book to begin reading again.

"Do you have her phone number anywhere? I'd like to tell her something." Sam sat up straighter as he readied himself for her reaction.

Beth dropped her book back to her stomach and screwed up her face. "What are you talking about? What has gotten into you—don't you think you have enough to do otherwise?" She made a sour face and shook her head.

Sam knew it would be hard to explain what he barely understood himself so instead didn't reply.

"Seriously?" she asked.

Sam stared back and tried to make the goofy expression he made when he was feeling inept that once made her laugh. It felt fake, but he hoped it might save him this time.

"Oh, good God. Fine. Hang on," she grumbled, but she failed to hide a glimmer of a smile as she sat up and placed her book, spine up on the coffee table. She groaned as she pulled herself from the couch and padded stocking footed into the kitchen.

"I texted it to you," she said as she peeked back in the room, both of them well practiced in keeping their voices to a whisper when Jack was finally asleep. "I'll be in the bathroom." As he opened her text message he heard the sound of the pipes, signaling the start of Beth's shower.

Sam stood up, hoping Jack was so tired from their daylong outing he would sleep through the night and well into the morning. He walked to the front door and quietly opened it before walking outside, leaving it partially ajar. It was unseasonably warm out, and stars and a crescent moon shone through the darkness. Sam sat down on the rusted lawn chair near the front door. He knew his body was tired from the beach day, but the thought of the call he was about to make perked up his energy. He held up his cell and touched the texted number, before putting it up to his ear. He hoped it wasn't too late for a call.

It rang only two times. "Hello?"

"Um, hi, Sarah?"

"Yeah, it is. Who is this?"

"You might not remember me, but I'm married to Beth. You worked with her quite a few years ago at the clothing shop at the mall? My name is Sam. We met a couple of times, a long time ago. You brought your mom along?" She must think him an idiot or a prankster.

The line was quiet for what seemed too long. "Um. Yeah, of course. I mean that was a helluva long time ago, ancient history. But I remember." She let out a rush of air. "I mean, I wasn't at my best. Then. Anyway, Beth left the shop before I did and we haven't been in touch. Is she okay?" Sam heard confusion dotting the conversation gaps.

The pause grew longer, and Sam was tempted to hang up. "Yeah I know. I called you on a whim. Beth's fine. Yeah, she's fine and I asked her for your number. It's just that I was reminded so much of your mom today. I don't know why, really, as I'd only met her a few times. What was her name?"

"You mean Gloria? You know this is weird, right?"

Sam could tell he caught her off guard. She sounded more than simply surprised, and he worried she was upset.

"Yes. That was it, Gloria," Sam said. "The first time, we were somewhere at a work party although I can't exactly remember where. You had told Sarah you had to bring her, or something like that. And, sorry, but you were complaining a lot about her. About your mother." He didn't intend to sound mean. "But I ended up talking to her because neither of us knew anyone else. We talked about how we could be third wheels together, all of you knowing each other from work. It happened two years in a row." He hesitated as he scratched a bug bite on his ankle. "Today, I met someone who reminded me of my conversations with her. With Gloria. She was so funny. Egged me on with some things and got me talking. I'm sure I talked way too much to her. To Gloria, those days." Like now, he thought, shaking his head and grimacing.

Sam stalled his rambling to allow Sarah to interject, but she didn't say anything. "I hadn't thought of her, although I remember hearing she died awhile back. I had noticed her obituary in the paper but Beth didn't remember her much. Not like I did." He knew he was prattling on but didn't think Sarah had hung up on him. He was glad Beth wasn't listening. Weird, after all, to call up someone so long after having them in your lives, and even then, barely knowing them.

"You know, it's funny," Sarah said, her voice softer. "Now that you say all that, I do remember her mentioning you. Back then I honestly didn't know who you were connected with, as Gloria was terrible with names and didn't remember either yours or Beth's. She had begun to get forgetful," she added, more quietly. "But she did talk about you all the way home. Oh, both times. I have to admit I teased her she had a boy crush." She laughed. "She called herself a wolf, which I had to ask if she meant a cougar. It was funny for a minute. But I was irritated with her so much in those days. More than anything I remember telling myself I should be relieved Gloria had found someone else to bother. I mean to chat with. Honestly, it makes me sad now to admit this. With her being dead and all. But I was annoyed she talked about you so much as if it had been her event, rather than mine. She had a better time than I did at those things. Frankly, she was better with people than me. Oh sorry, more than you need to know. Let's just say we had our issues."

Sam was not eager for another uncomfortable silence, so he blurted, "Well, again, I'm sorry about her dying and all," regretting the few words he chose. "I'm sorry."

"Oh, it's okay. She was a kick in the ass, I was too fucked up with my own stuff to appreciate it then. But she died awhile back. Why now? I mean why are you calling me after all this time?" Sarah didn't sound as if she was accusing him of anything, but as if she was trying to understand.

"No, right. Really. We should have called or sent a card. No excuses but our life got busy. We have a little kid now and we never seem to get to things like we mean to. You know like fixing a wobbly table." He knew he should get off the phone before he made a complete ass of himself.

"Oh, it's okay, I don't mean it like that. It's just . . . I'm sorry. It's weird to have you call. Gloria and I finally got close in her last two years. So actually, her death was oddly harder than I would have ever imagined."

"So," Sam hesitated again. Trying to think how to put it into words. "I saw this woman today who for whatever reason made me think of your mom. Of Gloria. She had this twinkle in her eye, and she connected with my son in this way that I could have seen Gloria doing. And there was a sadness about her. She mentioned her son. Well, my son Jack, reminded her of her son when he was little. But I could tell she was sad. Like she missed her son, but I don't know anything about him or if he's around or dead or whatever. But it also reminded me of Gloria because she had told me about being sad about not being close to her son. I guess that's your brother."

"Ted? Gloria talked about Ted? To you? Now, that's weird."

"You know, Sarah. Sometimes I think." He stopped, knowing it would sound sappy. "I think once in a while we tell people things, people who are more like strangers to us, that we might not tell those who are closer. Don't you think? And maybe it makes us feel sad. But then in another way it's kind of nice." He was glad again that Beth wasn't listening—he wasn't in the mood to be called Dr. Philosopher.

"Yeah, I guess."

"I should go," Sam said. "I know this has been a little weird. I only wanted you to know I was thinking of her. Gloria. Remembering her. It made me smile, and I wanted you to know. That's all. And, sorry for never sending a card or calling earlier."

The phone line was quiet. "Thanks, Sam. I mean, yeah it was a little out of the blue. Odd maybe. But honestly, it is nice to talk about Gloria. Especially from someone who noticed that side of her. She was funnier than hell. I learned that almost too late."

Sam ended the call and set his phone down on the porch railing. He closed his eyes. He was sure he could hear crickets. He could almost feel the tingling of the icy water on his feet. He remembered Jack's smile when the woman sat down in the water next to him. What a day, he thought.

Forgotten

"DO YOU EVER wonder if you unknowingly abandoned someone?" Jason flicked his glass, releasing soft tinkles from slowly melting ice cubes in his ginger ale.

"What, you mean like your kids?" Mary asked.

Jason rolled his eyes and vaguely shook his head. "No. Not my kids." He was irritated, more than once he had mentioned to Mary how he had no kids. Or a partner. "Professionally. You know, like what you do every day?" While she was a close colleague and had a reputation to be a well-loved therapist, he did not know how she could sometimes be denser than a volume of *The Brothers Karamazov*

"Oh, sure. I figure we all do. It is the baggage that goes with our work, don't you think?" Mary's brown eyes fixed on him, as if she finally interpreted his cry for a moment from her out of all those hours she exquisitely doled out to others.

She reached her hand out and encircled the wine glass stem displaying perfectly manicured glossy colorless fingernails, took her eyes off him and sipped the deep red slowly. She sighed, reset the glass on the table, and looked across the room. She closed her eyes briefly as if to escape the low scale suburban bar where Jason imagined bad karaoke debuted later at night, the owner's effort to entice locals into night life.

She opened her eyes. "Anyway, it's Friday. Let's move on. What are your weekend plans?"

Jason stared at her but forced himself not to shake his head in frustration, piqued at her not to wonder why he had asked the question. He knew he shouldn't blame Mary for his crappy mood. He had been haunted by a new worry since opening the weird letter from the mother of a student from long ago, forwarded to him from his previous employer. He remembered the boy, Paul. Jason surprised friends by his eccentric memory of trivial details that mostly didn't matter. He had once reluctantly, but successfully named each teacher and most students, first and last names, from his elementary school days when challenged at some party. He remarked cynically how this skill did nothing to further his life as an adult. Earlier that morning he had tried to ignore the unsettled feeling provoked by the letter. He had hoped this Friday night drink date with Mary could be the time to unwrap it, only now understanding how mistaken he had been.

"I don't know," Jason answered. This topic of weekend plans was as scintillating to him as discussing a weather forecast. Weekends were simply time to catch up before another Monday surged upon him. His usual: a movie or two, some reading, grocery shopping, and laundry. An occasional visit with a friend. Rarely these days a date. Nothing to waste on a minute of discussion. Nor did he care to hear about Mary's industrious weekend plans with her seemingly perfect, wealthy boyfriend. Yes, he knew she wanted to tell him about some planned hike to a stupendous peak with a breathtaking view and wine tasting at the best wine cellar in Yamhill Valley, or something equally magnificent.

Mary got the hint he was not interested in discussing weekend plans, and the discussion fizzled. Voices from the foursome in the table next to them rose loudly in their apparent drunkenness. Jason looked over to see one of the women dripping beer as she ineffectively poured drinks from a pitcher into each of her companion's glasses. He looked toward the bar to a server and tried to share his "I'm so sorry some people are assholes" look. He was glad he and Mary had enough time together before the increase in background noise and their trivial conversation so he could politely call it a night.

He drained the last of his drink, slurping the final sips to suck the liquid through mostly melted ice cubes, crunching the remaining icy bits. After setting his glass down, he turned to pull his jacket from the back of his chair and gathered it under his arm. His ancient GORE-TEX coat crinkled as he smashed it to his body.

"I'm beat," he said, lying, as he rose and looked down at Mary. He grabbed the ticket from the table. "My treat."

"Sure, oh, thanks," Mary replied. He knew he should wait until she finished her drink, but if she didn't want to examine the crud stuck in his brain he would expedite his exit. As if to confirm her lack of concern by his departure, Mary had already pulled her phone out of her purse and was swiping across its face. Jason hesitated before assuming she had nothing to add. "See you next week."

"Sounds good," he heard her say as he made his way to the till.

IT WAS STILL early as Jason headed outside into the late spring evening. He appreciated the approach of summer as it extended daylight into after work hours. He felt a lifting of his clients' psyches as well, as if an abundance of light made it a smidgen easier to deal with life's challenges. He ignored his parked car and walked. To stroll and think. He often advised clients to walk to enhance blood flow and oxygen movement to the brain and help tease apart worries and fears that fester, knotted up and entombed inside. One would think he was a compulsive exerciser based on how frequently he offered this tip to his clients, but he was his own worst enemy as he too often huddled inside, focused on news channels or movies he'd seen many times before. Tonight, though, he would walk. He headed along the newly poured sidewalk, curious if it might lead to a path around the lake he knew to be nearby. Manmade, he was certain, too pristine and perfectly shaped to be natural. Within a few blocks he approached the water, wooden benches neatly dotted its perimeter, predictable and staid rather than welcoming. His spirit needed wildness, not perfection on this night.

Jason had been stunned after he opened the letter. He'd hurriedly grabbed a few pieces of unopened mail at work to read at home the previous evening but was too tired to give any of it a second thought, leaving it in his car. Earlier that morning, only hours ago, he chastised himself for ever agreeing to take seven clients on Friday, making it his busiest day. He felt guilty but hoped one or two might drop as summer progressed. As much as he should hustle in to the office, his curiosity had finally gotten the best of him as he only then noticed his previous employer's return address scratched on one of the envelopes, compelling him to open it after he parked his car at work. Inside the envelope was a smaller one with his name and an old work address written in perfect cursive writing.

He released the seat control to gain more leg room, opened the smaller envelope, and began to read. Nausea crept in with each paragraph, exploding into a gut punch by the time he finished the final sentence of the letter. Shades of orange and yellow filtered through the car windows from the beginnings of a gorgeous sunrise, contradicting the letter's alarming message.

Paul's name sounded familiar at first, but it wasn't until he had finished reading the letter when he could fully match the name with the face. The boy had been but a kid, barely into his teen years when he attended his class. He imagined that more than a decade had passed since, elapsed time in which he had not given the kid a second thought, even though he had been one of his favorites. If he had not received the letter, Jason might have someday luxuriously imagined where life had taken him, or possibly not. Quiet, sensitive, smart. Difficult for some to understand and never with close friends. Not once a trouble maker. Now, Jason was startled and confused with the inconsistency of then and now.

He groaned as he jammed the letter and remaining mail into his pack and hustled from the car to the office, the vibrant colors now faded into muted morning light, knowing he would be forced to begin his first appointment without a cup of coffee. He shrugged as he pushed open the office door and hesitated in the waiting room.

"I will only be a minute," he said to the client sitting stoically with his chin resting on arms as they perched on his thighs. This appointment was often his most difficult and normally he liked to give himself a few minutes to prepare, even though the client requested to meet so early, always before the man's work shift. Jason pulled himself together, compartmentalizing his brain—something he hated doing even if he did it often.

It was more than two hours later when he was able to brew himself a cup of coffee. Left with twenty minutes before his next client, he unlocked his file drawer. It was easy enough to find his private notes from all those years ago in the journal he kept only for himself, back when he was trying to figure out what he might next do. He had no clue then about HIPPA or client privacy requirements that now rule his professional life.

But now, what felt like days later but merely hours, he was striding at a pace he could not keep up with. His armpits felt soggy and he slowed his speed and pulled his cotton shirt away at both underarms, knowing without looking how sweaty his polo was. "Well, damn," he muttered through heavy breathing, sensing a slow untangling of the confusing feelings that had amplified throughout his day. *He needed to follow his own advice more often.* He hoped he wouldn't develop blisters on top of everything else.

He had finally reached the path that circled the lake and Jason hesitated before walking clockwise in the opposite direction from a cluster of teens hanging out with skateboards. *Space, he needed space.* Rather than process the letter's contents perhaps it was best to forget it all. It wasn't like he was supposed to be the kid's savior, he argued, only an underpaid teacher trying to give kids an education. Mary, much more experienced than he, often chided him to set firmer client *boundaries*, usually putting the word in finger quotes. He thought her adding the quotes made it seem more like a joke or impossibility, rather than actual advice. Then, next she would usually tell him not to take things personally. Yet—how did one not take it personally when it all mattered? When deep down he cared, even if one client claimed he didn't give a damn about him. Jason walked faster again even though the pain gnawed at his gut. Yes, this was perfect: to create physical pain to match what was hijacking his emotions.

The letter's overarching message had continued to hover over him throughout that day, and although he didn't remember its exact details, he knew Paul's mother had not accused him of failing her son. Jason consoled himself—the burden he felt of failure was self-induced. The sweating, heavy breathing and now the lake's serenity, even if the lake was lined with cement, helped him process it. He only then realized that Paul's mother's intention was solely to share her sadness with someone. A human who might remember and care. *Why him?*

He stopped suddenly and pulled the letter out of his jacket pocket. As he reread it, its intention was confirmed: this mother was sharing her despondency in failing her child. He closed his eyes and crumpled the letter, squeezing it into a tiny paper ball. He no longer needed the letter to remember what had happened to the boy and jammed the tight wad back into his jacket pocket. As he neared a trash can Jason ignored the impulse to unload it, and walked on to a viewpoint where he rested the weight of his upper body on the rail and stared at the pond water, its fountains squirting streams into the air. Across the lake he could barely make out the gathering of teen boys, kicking skateboards between them.

He thought back to what he could remember about Paul. Quiet unless spoken to, or if asked about something he had read recently. Jason knew kids teased him but he had always thought it incidental and it didn't seem to bother the kid. Paul was a voracious reader, selecting content Jason never would have touched at that age, and Paul would smile when Jason reminded the class about the gift of reading above most else. Now that advice seemed like a worthless answer to life. If any of this murder accusation is true—what hope does that give anyone in predicting any kids' outcomes in the future?

THE HALF-MOON WAS rising as the sun began to set behind the coastal mountains as he completed the full circle around the lake. For a split second Jason teased himself with an invitation to drive to the coast to spend the night on the beach, a spontaneous act mostly foreign to him. It was warm enough to make it through the night with a jacket, hanging out with the sand fleas, building a bon fire. A whiskey would be nice except he knew he wouldn't. No, he wouldn't do any of that.

He felt removed from place, briefly challenged to remember how to get back to the bar and his car. The pain in his gut had fully resolved so he increased his pace again, trying to ignore how bone-tired he now felt. The thought of driving the few miles home to his empty apartment exhausted him further. Yes, he would return to his weekend routine, strangely always eagerly anticipating after doing so heading into a fresh Monday morning.

Jason was within a block of his car when he stopped next to a dumpster on the corner. He reached into his pocket and stuffed the crumpled paper into the crack under the dumpster's locked lid, cramming his fingers under the locked chain. He knew he wouldn't stop thinking about Paul, wondering what lay ahead for him, imagining what other kids he might have failed. He had been naïve to expect that each kid would move ahead, grow up and prosper. But now—he was older and barely wiser. He understood what little he might be able to change and how massive was the baggage beyond his control, yet compassion was the single thing he'd hold on to forever. Maybe he was right and Mary was so very wrong.

Jason pulled his keys out of the pocket of his khakis, and out of habit, looked for anyone lurking nearby before he opened his door. He got in and pulled the door closed quietly and turned his key in the ignition before opening his window. The local oldies radio station blared on, the one he was embarrassed to admit to be his favorite. "You just call out my name . . ." streamed from his open window. He turned down the volume before pulling his car into the street, brushing off the tears as they dripped down his cheek. He was glad it was Friday. Monday morning, he would return his journal to the locked file drawer and move on. All tucked back into that place of experience.

Lost Opportunities

MONICA HAD NOT been surprised. She always believed her ex-husband Frank would die before he hit fifty, well before he was old enough to draw his first social security check. He proved her wrong in that. A month after his death, she felt its finality for the first time. The bundles of anger, accrued over years, made her unable to feel much of anything except an odd sense of relief when first hearing news of his death.

In the past day a new feeling took up real estate in her spirit. She was rarely impulsive, not like Frank, but first thing earlier in the morning she had unpredictably called in sick to work. Now she headed out to the small town west of Portland where the five of them had once made their home.

In the years passed since her family lived in the house near the river, the town had changed to something almost unrecognizable to her. Yet, the new roads, intersections, and mini malls did not deter her seemingly automatic navigation to this old spot. Monica parked her car on the street across from the driveway and turned off her engine to peer through shrubs defining the edge of the property at the house. Its wooden frame's shabbiness reminded her of its broken dishwasher and her unanswered calls to the landlord. She wondered how many other families had lived here since then until something else nudged them forward, or if one of them made the big leap into home ownership, buying it outright.

Why was it only now as she spied on their old house as if an intruder, that she felt compassion for Frank? She had needed time to let his death sink in and she knew there was only now a finality in it—he was gone, leaving their life together fully in the past. Different than the old days when they fought and all she could think about was how to save herself and the kids, ignoring the loss of her own dreams. In the last few years she had half-heartedly accepted the part she had played in their discord, albeit small she asserted. But back then as they lived here on River

View Road, she and Frank were caught in isolated quagmires. They trudged through separate, parallel journeys too often antagonized by each other's presence—she saw only her side of the bog. In the ensuing years when she was no longer affected by his idiotic decisions, his name only occasionally bubbled to the surface by one of the kids. Should she feel badly now at not helping her kids continue their relationship with their dad?

She did not intend to discuss any of this now with her grown kids, it was all water under the bridge. Before Frank died, Annie was the only one of the three who had continued a relationship with him. They were old enough to craft their own stories about how much their parents did or didn't screw them up. Someday they might acknowledge all the little things she did for them, making sure they went to school, had food to eat, clean clothes to wear. They probably still took those things for granted, but maybe someday they'd get it, perhaps if they ever had kids of their own.

Yes, she had first felt an odd sense of relief when she heard Frank had died, and it wasn't until driving home from the memorial service that she sensed a stab of guilt. The next day she felt sad. It wasn't until this past week that, for the first time, she didn't feel angry about all the things he never did, or sad about never reconciling like the kids wanted when they were younger. The cleverly wrapped packages of frustration and anger, sealed and piling up for years, were strangely, slowly dissolving. Part of her wanted them back: it was easier to be angry than sad. Was she downhearted because she didn't know what his life was at its end? Monica wondered if Annie knew, but she hadn't been able to ask her youngest daughter this question. She and Annie had their own troubles.

Monica spied a man walking along the shoulder of the road. He hesitated before moving within earshot of her car. He kept his eye on his dog as it sniffed at the weeds across the street before stopping to lift his leg at the base of the mailbox.

"Something I can help you with?" he asked, taking his eyes off the dog to look suspiciously at her.

The man probably thought she was casing out the place, and Monica laughed out loud at such craziness. Her laugh so quickly tailed her emotional journey of memories that it sounded maniacal, and was weirdly punctuated by escaping tears. She was embarrassed. Sure, she may have threatened Frank a few times in those difficult years, but deep down she was timid and could never have hit him or thrown as much as a potholder at him.

"Oh no, I'm sorry," Monica choked out. "We once lived on this street and I was remembering. That's all." She turned away from the man to wipe her eye with her shirt sleeve. He was keeping a safe distance from her either because he was sure she was kooky or, simply to keep the dog within sight.

"Oh, okay," he said, hesitantly.

Monica pasted a smile to her face, and hoped he would move along. He looked back at her expectantly, as if he wanted to say something more, but instead turned and crossed the street.

"C'mon, Sarg," he said and whistled to the dog, a big black lab that lumbered as it walked. Monica watched them walk together back down the street.

She unbuckled her seat belt, unrolled all four windows, and slouched back. Although emotionally exhausted, she also felt strangely at peace. With the anger extinguished, it was as if finally floodgates jarred open, releasing memories. She could only then feel regretful. Freed from anger she could reminisce back before pain became a constant companion in their lives together. To think back to the first time she saw Frank, the first time they talked, the first time they had sex. Details locked inside delivering her a past that had felt lost, but perhaps only hidden.

He was gone, and she did feel sad. Frank would never again wander in or around the edges of her life, except as a memory. Her brain had finally cut through the poisonous crust that had built up. Would the memories dim, rework themselves entirely or stimulate others, allowing her to retrieve only the good of their past?

Monica knew she couldn't process this on the street that triggered so many bad times with Frank. She fastened her seat belt and drove without flipping on talk shows or music to get her off track, thankful for the innate ability to get from point A to point B with little conscious thought. She headed toward Southeast Portland without at first knowing why, until she pulled her car into the parking lot of Oaks Park. Although the amusement rides were open for the season, this day lacked the frenzy of summertime visits. She hadn't been here in years.

Of course she knew why her past dragged her here. She locked her doors, opened her windows a crack, and closed her eyes, resting her head back against the seat.

"I'VE SEEN YOU before," Frank had said to her that first Sunday afternoon.

Susan, her only friend at work, had begged Monica to join her at the company picnic. Monica had only worked at the automotive store for a few weeks and had no interest in getting to know her coworkers better. It was hard enough to work eight hours a day, five days a week doing something she struggled to understand, even if it allowed her to improve her accounting skills. But Susan was kind to her in those first few weeks and helped her understand new work expectations, only recently finishing a two-year college degree. And yet, as soon as they arrived at Oaks Park, one of the men asked Susan to join him on the roller coaster. The duo invited her but she wasn't interested in serving as a tagalong only to throw up in one of their laps. Instead, Monica grabbed a paper cup of lemonade from the group picnic area and moved to a bench nearby to sip the sickly sweet drink. She didn't care if she sat alone in the midst of others who were busy meeting wives and kids.

A few minutes later Frank wandered over. He looked familiar to her although she wouldn't have placed him if she passed him on the street, a good ten years older than her and ruggedly handsome. Looking back now, if alcohol had been served back then she doubted they would have hit it off as she had been raised by teetotalers. But that all came later. Frank introduced himself and asked her if she had ever roller skated before in the big pavilion, nodding his head toward the white building in the distance. When Monica said she hadn't, he quickly added that they'd have to go some time, as he released a broad smile. He wore work boots, even on this summer day, and bits of black grease streaked between his elbows and wrists. His thumbs and fingers straddled either side of the waist band of his jeans as he smiled back at her.

"Yeah, I work back mostly in the warehouse," Frank said. "You know, resupplying shelves, and sometimes putting orders together. But not for long, no, not me." Monica had looked at him curiously. "Nope, I've got big plans, trust me," he had said louder. He sported a sweet smile and a lot of enthusiasm. His cheeks stretched wide and a dimple popped out in the middle of one.

Reliving the memory roused Monica, and she opened her eyes and stretched her arms high to touch the ceiling before wiping the newly forming layer of sweat from her forehead. She grabbed her purse and shoved her cell phone inside, rolled up her windows, and opened the car door. If only she'd known what a line he had fed her that first day. A statement that would morph and breed others, later welcoming her to what she believed to be Frank's World of Fantasy. Yes, that was the issue and Monica had been late to realize it. Frank never understood how far outside of reality he resided much of the time.

Monica grabbed her sweater and car keys before locking the door, and wandered past the turnstile into the park. Ahead of her the trembling cottonwood leaves beckoned. Yes, she did believe him at first. He was confident and convincing about his grand plans. And she had to admit now, he was cute in his strangely confident, swaggering way.

She had little previous experience with men before Frank, having had only one boyfriend in high school. This new attention from a man caught her off guard. That day at Oak's Park they had continued to talk for a while until Susan tired of the rollercoaster and wandered back to find her. Susan's eyes first widened before she sent Monica a teasing smile, she had once tried to get her to double date but Monica had flatly refused. She told Susan she didn't want anyone at work to know anything about her private life, not admitting to Susan her hesitation was because of her inexperience with men. Monica returned Susan's smile with a scowl.

"Fine. I'm getting something to eat," Susan said and sulked off to the free food as she pulled a tube of lipstick out of her purse.

"It's been great chatting with you, Monica," Frank had said next. He looked at his watch. "I've got to run, but maybe we do it again? Like after work. Maybe next Friday?"

Monica felt her face redden but she was delightfully surprised, not used to attention from men, especially an older handsome man. Frank smiled at her. She didn't know what to say, but was relieved Susan had left.

"Yes, that'd be great," she sputtered.

Frank continued on as if he'd been certain she would agree. "I'll plan on getting you after work then. We can go get a bite." Before Monica knew it, he turned, nodded to someone in the crowd, and headed to the parking lot.

As she reminisced, Monica strolled through the quiet amusement park until she arrived at a trail near the cottonwood trees, no rude cyclists or loitering pedestrians to watch out for on this day. She stopped to look out at the muddiness of the river, across to the hills of Southwest Portland and the few houseboats moored in place with docks cabled together. The sounds of screams drifted from the roller coaster, but mostly it was quiet. She shivered in the breeze but didn't think to put on the sweater she held under her arm.

"I was so naïve," she muttered, thinking about how soon she and Frank had sex.

She knew little and when it was over so quickly and hurt so much she figured that first night that was all it was supposed to be. Soon after she learned how much better it could be, and she should give Frank some credit for helping her do that—surprised he was that she knew so little. It wasn't like she'd had a mother or girlfriends who had ever told her anything else, and she'd never been curious or brave enough to read the books and magazines she learned about later. Unfortunately for them, the whole package followed too soon after, pregnancy, shot gun wedding, two more kids. "I've forgotten so much," she told the river. But she had loved him, way back then in those earliest days. How had she forgotten so much? He drank little in those first years nor was he yet frustrated by the way life happened at him. All that came later. He had even been a good dad at first, she was sure of it. She had loved watching the way he was with Annie when she was a kid—and the adventures they'd shared in those early years. If only they'd had longer to first be a couple—she only now wondered if that might have made a difference?

Monica dropped her purse and sweater to the ground, and pulled her hair back with her hands as she bent slightly backward and looked to the sky. Maybe she could have done something different to have kept that bit of love and the beginnings of that first sense of family alive. *Where did it go?* For the first time since learning about Frank's death Monica fully grieved. She grieved that he had met the end of his life. This man, the only man who had known her through those earliest years was gone. Through all the sadness and anger, she felt only now that a bit of her died with him—this little piece that nobody else knew.

She picked up her purse and sweater, tucked them both under her arm again, and walked quickly toward delighted screams. She spotted the ticket stand and opened her purse to withdraw a five-dollar bill. When she neared the stand it appeared unoccupied, so she wandered on to the Ferris wheel. It was at a standstill and looked desolate until she spotted an attendant jogging toward her.

"Sorry if you've been waiting. This time of year, I have three rides to operate." He wrinkled up his youthful face in a wordless apology. If Monica was his mother she would tell him to wash his face and hands. "Ticket?"

"Oh, no," Monica said. "I didn't see anyone selling them. Will you take this?"

The man looked around. "No, I can't take cash, sorry. Ma'am." He hesitated before releasing a half-hearted smile. "But, you know the day is so slow. They probably left early," and he nodded toward the booth. "Here, just go ahead." He opened the chain and gestured her toward the seat nearest the ground, looking behind him toward the ticket stand again.

Monica was startled. Now she wasn't sure she wanted to ride on the wheel, but felt compelled after receiving the kind gesture. She gathered her things closer to her body, stepped up toward the seat, and snuggled herself down into its middle. The plastic of the seat had small tears in it and she wondered if they ever maintained the ride, but tried to put the thought out of her mind. The man brought down the bar and moved back to set it in motion.

She grabbed onto the bar with both hands. A memory returned to her about the time she and Frank had returned to the park when the kids were little. The two older kids rode together in one seat and she and Frank had tucked little Annie in between them. Annie had insisted on wearing her favorite red dress, and her skirt billowed in the gust created by the wheel. But now, as the Ferris wheel gently lifted Monica up into the air, warm tears dripped down her cheeks.

"Oh, Frank, you devil!" Monica yelled.

Then, she laughed out loud, silencing her tears. There were no people around to hear. As the car thrust upward, she gazed first across, and then as the wheel moved upward, down at the cottonwoods, the river, and across the valley toward the barely visible Mt. Hood.

"Oh, Frank," she said, quietly this time. She began to cry again. The Ferris wheel continued its path upward, and she again grabbed the bar in front of her tightly, her chest thumping as if she was riding for the first time. The clouds billowed fluffy and white above her in the softening daylight.

"I know," she heard. Monica was certain of the voice. The car crested at the top of the wheel, and her stomach tickled as it dropped her softly back down toward the ground. Her tears dried during the next wheel revolution, new sensations of tranquility seeping into her heart. Finally, the chair clunked to a stop, and the young man unfastened the bar. Distracted, she nodded in thanks and walked toward the parking lot.

Monica pulled her phone from her purse, and stood still, first hesitating before selecting a number.

"Hi Annie. I mean, Anne" she said. "It's Mom."

The Thing that Changed Everything

SHE HAD NEVER seen a dead body before. Three decades of life almost lived, and not one corpse witnessed, a bit surprising given the amount of time she'd spent fishing. Most seasons she would hear about some local, drowned or lost at sea. Maybe it was because most of those bodies were never found or had decomposed beyond recognition. No, it felt shocking to her that after living a mostly boring, small-town life that her first dead body was someone murdered, or so spun the rumor mill. Call Celia naïve, but she'd been around long enough to know a rumor was simply a rumor, rarely something you should hedge a bet on.

At first when she spied the body she thought it was just an old guy sleeping on the street, although that in itself would be uncommon in this town. If that was all it was, she's sure she would have kept walking since it was dark out and she needed to get home. Not that she ever felt unsafe on these streets, not like she did when visiting Seattle or Portland. But as she began to pass the crumpled figure, not noticing at first it was two not one, sirens rang out from a few blocks away. She hesitated, looking around to see who might have called the cops. Someone more observant to tell the difference between a corpse and a drunk, or maybe the person involved in whatever had happened. Now, weeks later what troubles her most is knowing that she might well have neglected reporting the body, leaving it to someone else to be a more compassionate bystander.

These many days later she couldn't get the image out of her mind. Blurry, to be sure, as she hadn't been close enough to even see a face. She so badly wanted to believe she knew what he looked like. Now, she was troubled by how unreliable her memory was: did she fictionalize the scene during this passing of time? As the sirens blared that night she was sucked into the action, moving closer to the figure on the ground, only then seeing it wasn't just one. Any street-smart person would have kept moving, rather than be wrongly accused. It was only as the ambulance neared, emitting sirens to join in concert with two patrol cars, did she understand. This wasn't simply some old guy sleeping off a hangover. Whoever he was, his journey looked to be nearly over, she felt certain.

She had wanted to move closer to the bodies, but the sirens and flashing lights had seemed to accelerate activity in the second figure. She thought she could see blood on the ground, just as a cop appeared out of nowhere and aggressively motioned her to move back. He looked afraid! She didn't think cops felt fear. The ambulance zoomed in and although her biggest achievement in medicine was CPR completion, she knew the man was a goner. She wanted a better view to see the EMT do her work. She imagined this responder would hold a lifeless wrist, and then as a last hope put her ear to the man's heart. Would she do all those things that actors did on TV emergency room shows? Celia willed the man to shake his head, push up from his elbows, and yell, "Get off me!" as if to only then realize the attention he'd drawn. The cops seemed involved in dealing with somebody else and Celia was suddenly overwhelmed by sadness, no longer curious, and could not wait to get away.

After they put the guy in the ambulance, the cop asked her the questions she expected, and she diligently offered her name and phone number, although the police never called her. It made her nervous not to know what they did with personal information: as if one day she would get a phone call accusing her of something. Maybe she should know more than what she told them. She had heard about stories like that—selective amnesia. That night she continued homeward and back to her house with the roommate who talked little, still unable to afford her own place even though she was nearly thirty years old. Still, she was relieved to have another person around. No, she did not share the story with this person who she hoped soon would no longer be a roommate, but later it was good to have company when the floor creaked and the tree branch rubbed against her window.

Since that night she comforted herself that she had not run from the scene. Although she knew this fact could not bring the man back, she insisted to herself she was not an apathetic passerby. It wasn't long, though, before this feeling ebbed away and she reprimanded herself: if someone else had not called the police would she have?

It was two days later she saw the incident mentioned in the online newspaper. She wasn't one to pick up a print copy, but ever since the night of the emergency she obsessively pored over the coastal news section online. She knew she could call the police station to try to learn more, but the thought made her nervous. She'd never had any encounters with cops, good or bad. Why should she care, they might wonder, unless she had more involvement than what she first reported? The news article was wimpy—so few lines of text dedicated to a life-ending event. The article confirmed the man's death and name along with one sentence about a person of interest, but nothing more. This article, rather than appeasing her, provoked her to obsess further about how and why it happened.

The details she remembered from the night seemed clearer, not having faded with the passing of time. Now she seemed to remember how the old man was wearing a pair of faded jeans with one of those old cowboy leather belts. He had a striped button-down shirt. Maybe he'd been out for a night on the town? And yet, she didn't remember knowing that the day after. She'd never seen a picture of the guy, but thought now he had looked a bit like her high school English teacher, the one who was awkward but kind. She knew that couldn't be. Her brain continued to spin details, and it left her feeling less sure about any of it.

Celia felt as though there must be a reason she had encountered this dead man. She did believe in fate, though she hated to admit it as she had been teased by friends when she was younger for often saying something was "meant to happen." Her friends got on her case, as if she believed nobody had the ability to change their lot in life. Celia tried to explain it was not what she meant, rather that fate had some hand in everything. As if one didn't know what small detail the universe might send to change up where your life was headed, like an arrow from Cupid's bow.

But she was not the one to call the cops nor would the outcome be different if she had not seen the dead guy in the first place, so she could not figure out what her lesson was supposed to be. Why wasn't her first dead body someone she loved, like her grandmother or a relative, hopefully an old one, so she could say, "It's all for the better. They had a long life." She didn't know enough about this man Frank to be able to say it was all for the better.

It had been sheer luck when she heard about his memorial service a week after he died. She felt guilty attending such a personal event so she planned to tell anyone who asked that she had met him at work once, a story nobody would be able to verify. Yet, as she entered the community center that Sunday afternoon, she did not get the feeling anyone would ask. It was not an event where attendees seemed to know one another. One guy spoke for a short time, but mostly the fifteen people or so gathered in hastily set up folding chairs kept to themselves. Celia sat in the back, and looked around blankly at others who sat stiffly, most still with their coats on, and wondered if there was family present? It was hard to tell. The guy speaking said he was a friend, although he showed little emotion. The event seemed so matter of fact. The man talked about how Frank liked to hang out and watch the ships go over the bar and was fascinated with the Astoria Column. It seemed odd to her for these to be the last words publicly about this man, this guy Frank. The man invited others to speak, but nobody seemed to take him up on the offer so he abruptly ended it.

Celia stood up and walked over to the drink table, feeling like an imposter as she tried to steady her hand and nonchalantly pour lemonade from a glass bottle into a paper cup. She wished there was coffee, although she knew it would be watery or bitter.

"How did you know Frank?" Somehow the man had sidled up to her without her noticing. *Damn.* She knew she should have slipped out the door as soon as he stopped talking.

She was no longer prepared to answer this question.

"Um, no, I didn't. I mean I didn't know him well." She tried to change the focus away from her. "What about you?" She wasn't sure why she had gotten a drink except it felt like the thing to do. She didn't even like lemonade.

"I knew him for many years, just around town," the man said. "But I would have liked to have known him better. He was the kind of guy that mostly kept to himself. Don't get me wrong—I'm sad he died. Like that." He hesitated and looked at Celia. "I'm Jim, by the way."

Celia felt overheated and wished she had taken her coat off earlier, but knew better than to remove it now as it would be one more thing to impede her escape. She reminded herself there was nothing she could have done to change the outcome, but she felt guilty not to tell Jim she had seen Frank on the street. The silence began to feel uncomfortable, and without anything else to say she blurted, "What did you mean about the Column?" As soon as the words were out she silently admonished herself. She wanted to escape, not make small talk.

"Frank seemed convinced for a while that gold was hidden there. You know, he had this side of him, the little I knew, that believed some big new opportunity would open up. I remember him telling me how he rented one of those metal detectors once and spent a weekend up on that hill looking for treasure. Can't imagine he ever found anything beyond a nickel or two. Who knows why he thought this?" Jim continued on but Celia stopped listening.

When he finally ran out of chatter she asked, "Do you know the time?" She knew it wouldn't matter what time he told her. "Nice to meet you Jim. I'm overdue for something. I'm sorry for what happened to him. To Frank."

"Sure," he said, and moved away from her toward the food as she headed to the door.

The cooler outside air provided relief to Celia, and yet she did not feel any of the closure she had hoped the service might provide. Instead, it created additional questions: why did someone spend money on lemonade and cookies, and yet nobody had stepped forth emoting love for this man? Maybe that was it. Someone should be devastated that this man had died, she told herself.

"HI. UM, JIM. I'm sorry I don't remember your last name?" It felt personal to call this man she knew only by first name, although she felt lucky to find his number listed in the event information online. Only in a small town would people feel safe enough to list their personal phone number.

Celia had suffered a week of mostly restless nights, nightmares laced with human bodies that oddly morphed into weird-looking animals. She knew she needed to do something, but had no idea what it might be. Then, in the middle of the night, she vaguely remembered a comment Jim made after the service, after she thought she had stopped listening.

"Yes," she said that morning on the phone, "I met you at the service for the man. Frank." She wanted to scream: the dead man. She forced herself to control her voice and steadied her left hand with her right by jamming the phone into her ear. *Was this what it felt like to go crazy?* "My name is Celia."

"Oh yes, I think I remember you. You're not the daughter, right? You live here in town?"

"Yes, I do, thanks." She was surprised to hear that Frank had a daughter. "You had said that Frank had a friend he visited sometimes. I don't think you said much about it, or maybe I've forgotten, I'm sorry." She hesitated, knowing she had been so eager to escape that she hadn't paid attention. She had thought then, incorrectly, that less time spent dwelling on anything about the man would help her forget about all of it faster. "It was a friend he visited sometimes. Or, I guess helped out or . . . ? I'm sorry I don't remember exactly." He must think her weird or nosy. Or both.

Yet, Jim spoke up, continuing in a friendly voice. "Oh yes, Frank's friend. Well it's an older man. He lives with someone who helps take care of him, I think. I don't know the exact address, but I can tell you precisely how to find it, up there on the hill." He then proceeded to explain what street it was on and what the house looked like.

"Have you met the man? Or the one he lives with?" Celia asked.

"No, I don't even know their names. Once I gave Frank a lift there after his car broke down. He never said much about it, but somehow it had come up that he visited him from time to time."

Celia hesitated. This was so little to go on, and she wanted to know more, even if she wasn't sure what she was searching for. "Thank you," she said reluctantly, wishing this time their conversation was longer.

"You bet. And, again I'm glad you could stop by last week. I'm sure Frank would have been pleased."

Celia set the phone down and snorted air out her nostrils. The dead man would be pleased. Ha! Not if he knew she was the one who ignored him. The one who would have walked right by leaving him on the dirty sidewalk. Though she had turned her back on her Christian roots even before she left her parents' house, vague teachings sometimes trickled back, clinging like toffee in her teeth. No, she told herself, shaking her head. This is not about making amends.

She stood, grabbed her hair tie off her wrist, and pulled her coarse, curly black hair into a clumsy pony tail. Strands hung down on either side of her face and she tried to push them back into the elastic. It was only ten in the morning but she'd been waiting since the middle of the night to act on this idea to call Jim. She grabbed her half cup of leftover coffee from the counter, set it in the microwave, and turned the dial for a full minute. She needed it scalding, even if it hurt going down. Things had been slower at work and she'd agreed to take some time off. Not that she could afford it but her lack of uninterrupted sleep was affecting her ability to think clearly, as if she was dreaming during her waking hours while exhaustion created unsolvable puzzles in her brain. She wished for the mellower days of before, knowing they weren't exactly easy. Before she had spotted the body.

She sat down on the folding chair near the front door, hunted for her sneakers on the floor, and tied her laces in double knots as she imagined her route.

AS CELIA NEARED the block, it was easy to identify which house Jim had described: gray weathered siding, front dirty white picket fence collapsing in a corner. A car in the driveway that looked as if it had been abandoned for years. She would have preferred calling ahead, but she did not even know the man's name. The mailbox listed a nameless, barely legible address. Her heart thumped loudly against her chest wall as she walked up the path toward the house. She ignored internal warnings that she could be walking into danger as she knew she had to get through this. It was the only next step.

Three concrete stairs led up to the door, and they were barren of anything except a rolled, plastic-wrapped advertisement. She picked up the advertisement and set it next to the wall of the house, and waited at the top landing, hoping she might hear something. Nothing. She ignored the doorbell, and knocked on the door four times, softly, nervously. Stopping to listen. This time, more boldly she rapped harder on the door, once, twice, several more. She put her ear to the door and then quickly backed off.

"Coming, coming!" she heard in the distance. Stomach acid seeped into places in Celia's gut where she was sure it should not go, and she shifted her weight from one foot to the other. Was she hungry after skipping breakfast or terrified? Anyone who knew her would be shocked by this act, rarely impulsive.

The door swung open and a wiry man with thinning gray hair peered at her. He stooped forward, and for a moment Celia worried he might lose his balance. He continued to stare at her, and Celia backed away from the door, speechless.

"Yes? What now?" He had on baggy sweatpants and slippers, and sounded irritated, like she had interrupted something.

"Hi. Uh, I wondered if you had a few minutes to talk?"

The man looked puzzled. "What? I can't hear you. And, well, I can't stand here all day, unless you want to pick me up here off the ground." Without another word the man turned away from her, leaving the door open, and retreated back into the house. Celia watched him hesitate before sitting in a plaid recliner across the room by the window. She looked around outside, worried that a neighbor might think she was here to harm or rob the old guy. Not knowing what else to do, she stepped inside the house, reached back and pulled the door closed and walked across the worn shag carpet toward him. The room smelled like mildew and old French fries. Across the small room was a pull-out couch, still unmade with sheets, and a coffee table holding dirty dishes.

"Who are you and what do you want? Before you sell me magazines you should know I hardly read. Oh, and I don't have a check book or cash, but go ahead, just lay it out, would you?" The man looked up at her. Celia spotted a chair near him but it was covered with clothes and did not look inviting, so she remained standing. "Hey, wait," he suddenly blurted. "I know who you are. Oh good. You came."

Celia was startled. She turned to look behind her thinking someone else had quietly followed her into the room. She wished she had left the front door open, feeling nervous to stupidly walk into some old guy's house, even if he seemed harmless. If not for safety, an open door might ventilate the room. She did not know what to say.

"Oh yeah," the man continued. "You're that friend of my daughter. You know my daughter visits, well not very much but she comes. She told me a friend of hers was moving out here. A friend would visit me."

Celia caught her breath. Her bizarre morning was now transitioning into an episode of *The Twilight Zone*. "Uh, no. I don't think so. I'm Celia."

"Celia," the man said, letting the esss sound languish before giving a hard "ya." "Not a name I've heard, I don't think. But it's lucky you found me because I didn't go to work today. I'll probably go tomorrow."

"Really?" Celia didn't want to sound as though she didn't believe him, so she added, "Where do you work?"

"Oh, you know, down at the docks. I move the boats around and, yeah, it's a lot of work but I've done it all my life, really. It's good, keeps me active."

She didn't want to make it obvious, but she eyed the walker on the other side of his chair.

"And I just need to warn you my son might be coming by but I haven't seen him in a few days. You probably know him, for all I know."

Celia decided to follow his lead, not sure whether what he said was truth or nonsense, but leaning toward the latter. "Your son?"

"Yeah, he's a good son. We had a bit of a falling out but he came back. That's what good sons do. Daughters too, I'd say."

"What's your son's name?" Celia asked, starting to feel like she needed to sit, but uncertain she should stay any longer, even if she needed to know about the guy's connection to Frank. *Why in the world was she there? She was absolutely batty.*

The man stared at her blankly and then confused, glancing away to look out the window. Then he looked back at her. "It's John. Yeah, it's John."

Celia was not one to join in on small talk, if this weird conversation could be defined as small talk. But she could not seem to help herself. "Well, when John comes, what do you do?"

"Oh, we talk, like this. Except he mostly talks. I listen. We talk about boats. Of course. Shipwrecks, you know. Oh, guy things." For the first time, the man smiled at her. "Yeah, there's lots of shipwrecks happening around here, it's a dangerous ocean, I'd say. You know, no, you probably don't. But we call it the Graveyard. Uh, the Graveyard of, um, of the Ocean. Oh, and treasures." Celia wanted to help him by sharing the word Pacific, but she caught her tongue. The word treasure triggered Celia, reminding her of Jim's gold discussion.

"Lots of things. Yeah, he's a good boy." He hesitated, one of his eyebrows and a corner of his mouth raised. He squinted and looked down at the floor. He looked back at Celia. "I'm sorry I forgot your name. It's been nice to visit but I need to get ready to go out soon. Thanks for telling me all those things and I'll be sure to think about them. We can talk again about things. But you don't need to bring the newspaper, you know, like my son does. Just so you know that. I can't really see it much. And nothing good to read in it anymore."

"Uh, well, I see," Celia replied, although she didn't. "Where does he live? Your son, John?"

"Oh, he lives around here. He's a good boy. Yes, he's a good boy."

"OK," Celia said, in a whisper. She wiped her eyes with her fists, as she felt disparate pieces slowly mending together.

She started to walk to the door, and then turned back to him. "I'm sorry, but I don't know your name."

"How could you forget such an easy one." He laughed for the first time. "Joseph. Joe is what my friends call me."

"Joe," Celia repeated. "If I come again, can I bring you something?"

"Oh, you don't need to bring me anything. My car is parked outside if I need supplies. Yeah, I just go get them. You go do your things. I have things to do too."

Celia didn't reply, but wiped her palms on her yoga pants. As she walked toward the door, she looked back to see if he was following her to the door, but Joe was slouched back in his chair and his eyes were closed.

As she opened the front door, she almost bumped into a middle-aged woman pulling keys out of her purse on the front landing.

"Who are you?" the woman asked rudely. "Can I help you?"

Celia moved away from the door, and replied softly. "I, I was visiting Joe." Celia felt as if she was busted for stealing something. "Does he live alone?"

"Joe? Hell no, thank God. Did he let you in?" The woman turned to pull the door closed. "I've got to talk to Derrick about that. Someday somebody's going to do something awful here, you mark my words."

"No," Celia said quickly. "A friend of mine told me to visit. But I don't know much about him. About Joe?" She hoped the woman might be a talker, for the second time she was reminded how never before had she wished this prior to this strange obsession of hers.

"Joe? He's mostly a good guy. But he is lucky as hell Derrick lives with him. You know, like one of those caregivers except he's only here at night. Joe's vet benefits cover some basics so he can still live alone. Well mostly alone. The guy would die if he had to go to one of those places." The woman looked at her and made a face and then rolled her eyes. "You, know. An old folks home."

"But he still drives and goes to work, and . . ." Celia realized how silly she sounded.

"Oh, honey, really? I mean, he did that twenty years ago. He barely leaves his house much these days, wanders outside a little bit, I guess. Derrick buys his groceries and between that and the Meals on Wheels ladies, he gets by."

Celia slapped her head. *How could she be so stupid?* "Oh, of course." She moved off the landing so the woman could pass by her. "His son? How often does his son come?"

The woman looked at her now as if she were a small child. "His son? He doesn't have a son, honey. As far as I know he's never had any family around. If he did they've either died or forgotten about him. He's lucky to have a house and Derrick, and occasional visits by people like me. Otherwise, who knows where he'd end up?"

Celia knew she should drop it but she couldn't stop herself. "Uh, I thought he said he had a son. Maybe named John?"

"Oh. He's probably talking about that guy. Oh, what's his name. An older guy. Not John. Charles or, yeah maybe Fred. Comes and visits him quite a lot. Seemed to be a big storyteller too. Not surprised he calls him his son. Next thing you know he will call you his daughter. I mean if you come again. Yeah, I haven't seen that guy Fred around for a few weeks, it seemed he'd usually come at least once or twice a week." She looked at her watch again.

"Could it be Frank?" Celia asked quietly.

"Yes. That's it. Now, I've got to go, really." The woman hoisted up her white stretch pants and put her key in the lock.

"Can I ask you?" Celia began, her voice wavered. "If I were to come by and bring him something. Joe. Is there something he'd like?"

The woman's impatient look broke into a grin. "Joe? You bet, that is easy. Pepsi. Not diet Coke." And as if in answer to a question Celia might ask, although she never would have thought to, she added, "He's not diabetic or anything, so it's fine." And with that she turned to face the door as if to avoid any more questions.

"I'll do that," Celia whispered to herself. She had been relieved to get out of the stale household air, and now it felt glorious to be free to walk along the sidewalk. Although her body was exhausted, her mind was ablaze. She felt settled, as if she finally had the answer to life's most complicated question.

As she walked along the street, heading back downhill, she could spot the Columbia River. She slowed her pace as she walked toward her apartment, first stopping at the city's only Safeway. She had not eaten all day and realized she was ravenous. Without thinking, she picked up a bag of pasta, jar of tomato sauce, and a donut from the bakery, and piled it into a hand cart. The store was quiet, and she headed to the express checkout. She began to put her items on the conveyor belt, and then retraced her steps to pause in front of the cooler at the head of the checker aisle. Celia shivered at the shock of cold air when she opened the cooler door. She looked at the various labels, and swiftly pulled out a bottle of Pepsi. She reached back in to grab a second container for good measure, before retreating back to the checkout stand.

Frank

FRANK KNEW HIS time was running out. He'd never been one to worry about his health, instead priding himself on how rarely he visited a doctor. Other than back when he'd gotten hurt at work and needed pills more than anything for pain. He had been working in the warehouse, back during those days they had lived on the river. A large crate had fallen on him and crushed his back. He had eventually gone to the ER, lying that it hadn't happened at work since nobody there seemed to believe that it had. But it had been years since he'd begged to refill that prescription, eventually learning to live with the pain.

Now was different, and he was smart enough to know something was going on inside him. He didn't need a doctor to tell him he spent a lifetime drinking too much, and what kind of toll that could take on a body. Frank dropped by the library earlier in the winter to use the computer, looking at pictures of unhealthy livers and all those signs somebody might be feeling. Yes, he pretty much knew his days were numbered and had come to terms with it. Recently he'd driven to all his favorite local places, even across the long bridge that crossed the mouth of the Columbia to climb up to the lighthouse perched on the cliffs. The short walk exhausted him but he stood out that day in the wind and rain, peering down to the surf as it crashed on the rocks far below. He would have been a guy to have manned a lighthouse long ago, he was sure.

It was the twenty in the parking lot that confirmed it all to him, though. There he was, minding his own business walking from the grocery store to his car when he saw its edge flapping in the bit of breeze that evening. He picked up his pace, his eyes darted around to make sure nobody else saw it. Lucky for him, most people had headed back home. Frank grunted as he bent down, his back always ached in that position, thinking he'd be lucky if it was a fiver. He could not believe it when he spotted the Andrew Jackson twenty. *Imagine that, twenty bucks in a goddamned parking lot.* He knew he could go back into the store and ask if someone dropped the bill, but come on, who would do that? No, far more sensible to pocket it.

It was then as Frank opened his car door and sat down in the driver seat that he bust out laughing. He laughed so hard his chest hurt. His treasure. He had finally found his damn treasure. About time. His damn luck it was certainly not the gold that would buy him and his mostly estranged family all that he had once imagined. Twenty bucks might buy dinner, dessert, and a beer.

He didn't even buckle up, distracted as he steered the car back to his apartment, wondering which restaurant to visit. Recently he had to scrimp to make it on his Social Security, no longer attempting to pick up odd jobs. He pulled his car into the apartment parking lot, and while he unlocked the front door to his place, he changed his mind. He laughed out loud again, and left his front door wide open as he hurriedly dug around in a drawer in the kitchen for an envelope. He hoped the address he had was the right one and felt lucky he had a stamp on hand. He did this all quickly as if he was afraid he'd change his mind, jamming the bill in the envelope before he painstakingly wrote her name and Seattle address on the outside. He set it on the counter and hoped he'd remember to drop it in the mailbox in the morning.

Later, when he was finally in bed, eager to get off his feet and relieve his swollen ankles, he wondered if he should have included a note. Maybe he'd write, "Dear Annie, I finally found it! And I give it all to you!" Then he'd have to add that ridiculous LOL like all the young people do. No, he decided, it's better for her just to think her old man was thinking about her.

The next day was beautiful, the sun rising up above the coastal mountains to the east, but Frank mostly hung around inside, even though he knew the weather would soon change to cold and gray. He didn't have energy to do much of anything this past week. His biggest accomplishment after he got up was to walk to the mailbox on the corner, and he chuckled again at this antic. *See, Monica, I still have it.* He hoped that his Annie would always know what she meant to him, even if mostly they didn't talk and if Monica seemed to hate him. Maybe someday Monica might remember the good they did once have together, long ago. He dozed through the day, turning on the TV for company.

Frank didn't have much appetite but ate leftover macaroni and cheese, just as the sun was about to set. He suddenly felt the urge to go out and see the Columbia. This once salmon-laden tributary brought him comfort, no matter what. He put his bowl in the sink and hesitated in front of the fridge. "Oh, what the hell," he muttered as he opened the door and grabbed a can of Budweiser from the bottom shelf. He was tempted to drive as he felt so tired, but knew it was just a few blocks to his favorite spot along the boardwalk. Not far from where those old fishing vessels from long ago might have moored. Out of habit he jammed his beer in a small brown paper bag, but knew nobody really cared anymore. He would force himself to wait till he saw the water to open it.

He neared the spot just as the sun was setting. It was perfect, and he took the beer out of the bag and pulled back the tab. Yes, perfect, he thought, swallowing the liquid, his poison. That he knew. He leaned against the railing and closed his eyes for a moment. It was all going to be okay. He was certain.

Loud shouting caused him to open his eyes. He might have even nodded off. Probably just some guys having too much Saturday night fun, he figured. Frank had never been much of a socialite, or loud when drunk. But those who were didn't rub him the wrong way like they did some. Whatever floats your boat, he felt. Then the shouting got louder, and he saw two guys getting into it, yelling and spitting and he didn't know what else as they neared him.

Frank didn't normally get involved in others' business, but he had been feeling peaceful and serene, and couldn't help himself. "Hey, keep it down a bit, okay?" The two guys, probably close to Annie's age he thought, seemed surprised to see him.

"Fuck off, old guy," one of them said. The other one, even though they had seemed to be at each other's throats only a moment before, shouted his agreement.

"Yeah! Mind your own fucking business." He sneered at Frank before turning to give the other guy a wicked smile.

"I don't mean no trouble. Just out enjoying the sunset. And my beer," Frank added.

The taller guy with the stocking cap veered over and stomped up to Frank, flicking his hand as he targeted the can of Bud.

"What'd you do that for?" Frank asked, as he watched the can fall to the ground. He couldn't understand what these young assholes would want with him. But suddenly he was so tired, and could almost only focus on his aching legs. Frank bent down to get his can from the ground, hoping to save some of the beer, when something heavy smashed across his head, and he was knocked fully to the sidewalk, lying on his belly. Frank wanted to say something. He wanted to ask why but he could not form the words.

"What the fuck are you doing?" he heard the other guy say, the words fading as he moved away from Frank.

"He deserved it, you heard him. Old fucker nobody probably even cares about." Frank felt a kick at his gut, and suddenly doubted that he would catch his breath ever again. "Let's get out of here!"

Then it was quiet, so quiet. Frank's head hurt, and if he opened his eyes, everything seemed to be blurry and spinning. He tried to think about the sunset. The water. It had all been so perfect. He thought he heard a yell from a distance, but it was too confusing to figure out. Then he felt the warmth of a body next to him. He forced his eyes open and although everything was blurry he saw feet clad in those hippie sandals Annie had once begged for. Rescued by a hippie, he thought. He would have smiled, but he couldn't seem to.

"It's okay, man. I'm here. I'm with you." The voice was quiet. Calming. He felt something touch his head and warmth circling his body. He wanted to tell the man. *My Annie. Take care of my Annie.* But he couldn't get the words out. Frank closed his eyes. His last thought was how comforting it felt to be near the River.

A Next Chapter

SHE DIDN'T KNOW this part of town. Truthfully, she didn't know any part of the town well but was grateful for her visit. She imagined this to be the bench, the right bench, next to a pink flowering dogwood. Late blossoms, she thought. The pink flowers of the dogwood were her favorite—she knew that wasn't by chance. Chance doesn't work like that, not real chance. She slowly crouched, putting her hand behind her to feel for the hard bench, and lowered herself to sit. Waiting. Marjorie was uncertain what might happen. With all that hadn't been said, and so little that was. Yet she believed. Even with all that had happened, she believed.

The air was cooling as it neared dinner time and the sun would be setting before long. Her mood made her feel as though the sun should be warm and shining, instead it hid behind darkening clouds and she began to imagine it might rain. Rain was second nature to coastal Oregonians and unlikely to surprise any of them when drops fell out of the sky. People here were used to getting wet.

She strained her eyes, wishing her vision was better but knowing she was lucky to still see as much as she did. Marjorie pulled her arms tight to her body, hugging her jacket close to her core to try to head off shivers that had begun. She wasn't sure if the trembling she felt was from excitement or fear of not knowing. To be afraid not to know more about the one she loved, had always loved, more than all else. *The park felt hushed.* She heard only a few birds in the distance, unsure if they were gulls or common crows. Not that it mattered to her which.

Then, a human shape appeared in the distance. She peered intently, squinting to discern if the blob looked familiar. She watched it move closer, spying a slight limp in its right leg, a hobble only she knew from that time long ago after a spill from a dirt bike. She had been the one to take him to the emergency room, one of dozens of times she learned something more about this son of hers. Her eyes remained glued to the shape as it approached, straining to recognize the shirt, the pants, the shoes. Yes! She spotted sandals, his signature footwear. The figure sped up, and then slowed, as if it didn't know if it wanted to arrive sooner or later.

Only then could she clearly see the face. Only then was she certain: it was him! Her love, her little boy. The one she had only recently learned she couldn't protect from the world. *Was he too gentle for society?* Then she identified his brown eyes, wide open, eyebrows raised. Was it in fear or surprise? Was he surprised she came, after the silence? Then he lowered his eyebrows and his nose, the crooked nose he got from his father, twitched. Only she knew how he sniffed regularly and she hoped he took care of his allergies, quickly reprimanding herself that her son was an adult. Then he smiled. Paul smiled and she forgot all else: worries, fears, hopes. He smiled at her, his eyes crinkled, and the right eye closed slightly like it did as if a half wink. It gave him a slightly unbalanced look, which she knew meant pleasure. Only she would know that. This mother of his.

Paul's steps slowed. Marjorie felt she could see his mind working as he tried to figure out what to do next. This son of hers. The one who thought before he talked, creating a silence others didn't know what to do with. But she did, this mother of his. Now he was a few feet away. She could clearly see the beard he had grown, trimmed neatly. His favorite washed Levi's so soft, soft T-shirt, touch important. He continued to smile, but hesitated as he stood in front of the bench a few feet from where she was sitting. And then he sat, looking straight in front of him, away from her. The gulls quieted, or the crows, and she was glad. Quietness helped. He continued to sit without speaking or looking directly at her. Then, abruptly, he rose. Her heart leapt in panic—would he leave? And yet, she remained silent as this time she would not be the one to decide for him. To speak for him. This was his turn and she would live with it. This adult son of hers.

Without looking at her, Paul moved his sandaled feet closer to her and hesitated before he sat again closer. Marjorie felt the pressure of his thighs gently next to hers. Without looking at him she could feel his head near but towering above hers. This big son, this grown son of hers. She glanced at him but he was staring at his hands as they clasped his thighs, his strong fingers. Marjorie looked away, toward the returning sounds of the gulls, knowing now they were gulls, and she was reminded of the ocean nearby. An ocean that had splashed on her toes and this son's toes, long ago.

Marjorie felt Paul's touch, and looked down at her left hand to see his warm dry fingers softly wrapped around it. She felt the roughness of his skin. She knew these fingernails to be bitten to the quick but the hand was warm and strong. She wondered if they had healed, these hands of his. She glanced at him, but he continued to stare ahead, as if mesmerized by the sights in the distance. He was smiling. Then she watched him close his eyes and felt his rib cage relax as it touched her torso ever so slightly. She sat backward and let her body relax to gently rest upon this tall man sitting next to her. This strong man, this son of hers. And she knew. She knew it would be OK.

Acknowledgements

Writing during the pandemic was essential for me. I thank Joan for stirring the earliest seed of this book during a pre-pandemic conversation as I waited for the bus one morning: does good sometimes come from bad?

Although Patty Montgomery is not here in person to celebrate the release of this book with me, as she has my others, I thank her for listening to my earliest ideas, and rooting for me when I signed the contract.

I will miss Kris forever. I won't forget the day I told her, before anyone else, what would happen in *Humanity's Grace*. And she got it.

My friends at Writers Table, meeting virtually during this past eighteen months, Maura, Leigh, Emily, Shelly, Michael, and Karen, helped me bring my manuscript to final form. Thank you for your friendship, feedback and co-creating our safe space.

The good folks at Bedazzled Ink have been loyal and respected friends. Thanks for understanding my stories, and helping me set them free.

Finally, thanks to Russ for being a listener, reader and supporter. I love you.

Dede Montgomery is the author of *My Music Man, Beyond the Ripples*, and *Then, Now and In-Between: Place, Memories and Loss in Oregon*. Dede is a 6th generation Oregonian and lives near Portland, Oregon. Learn more at https://dedemontgomery.com

Aim your phone's camera at the QR Code.

CPSIA information can be obtained
at www.ICGtesting.com
Printed in the USA
FSHW011534231221
87127FS